FOLLOW YOUR DREAMS

Nov 2012
With Best Wishes
and
Kindest Regards.

[handwritten signatures]

Also by Larry B. Gildersleeve
Dancing Alone Without Music

FOLLOW YOUR DREAMS

A Novel

Larry B. Gildersleeve

Published by Adelaide Holdings, LLC

Larry B. Gildersleeve
P.O. Box 9878
Bowling Green, KY 42102
www.larrygildersleeve.com

Adelaide Holdings, LLC
P.O. Box 9878
Bowling Green, KY 42102

First Edition: July 2017

Library of Congress Control Number: 2017908724

ISBN-10: 0997370017
ISBN-13: 9780997370089
ISBN: 978-0-9973700-1-0

Printed in the United States of America

This book is dedicated to every woman who followed her dreams.

Go confidently in the direction of your dreams. Live the life you've imagined.

— HENRY DAVID THOREAU

*All the flowers of all the tomorrows are in the seeds
of today.*

— *INDIAN PROVERB*

Marla Taylor regarded Josephine Gilpin as the most remarkable woman she'd ever met.

The challenge for Marla had been to translate her feelings into words as she prepared to be the main speaker at a ceremony honoring Jo. Hundreds of millions of dollars, and Jo's entrepreneurial leadership and her generosity, would be discussed in front of at least two thousand people on a beautiful spring day near Lexington, Kentucky in April, 2017.

Jo Gilpin had directly impacted the lives of thousands of people, and many in the audience had known the woman they were honoring for decades. Despite their closeness in age, growing up in the same small town in Kentucky, Marla had known Jo for only a matter of months. And they had been drawn together for a different reason.

The two women discovered they had much in common, including their Christian faith and the life challenges each had endured that tested the strength of their beliefs. But in so many ways, they couldn't have been less alike. They had been born in different hemispheres and into vastly different circumstances. One had been risk-adverse, personally and professionally; the other had taken risks all her life. But when they finally met, they developed a shared desire to accomplish something they believed could positively affect the lives of countless women. And they had a limited time to accomplish their task.

As Marla nervously approached the podium, and gazed out at the crowd overflowing the venue, her mind turned back to how it all began – with a meeting in the office of her husband Ben.

August 9, 2016

"May I interrupt for a few minutes?"

Ben Taylor was working in his office when he looked up and saw Jennings standing in the doorway. Despite the heat outside, Jennings wore his suit coat as he did every day in every season. Although workplace fashion had evolved to informality almost everywhere else, "coat and tie" was still their executive dress code, with jackets worn at the office when meeting with guests, and for business events away from the office. Ben's navy blazer was hanging on the coat rack in the corner next to the bookcase. Even though he didn't participate, Jennings had years ago introduced casual Friday, which only meant ties were left at home.

"Of course," Ben answered, standing.

The truth is, Ben cherished every moment spent with Jennings Eldridge. His soft-spoken voice and courtly mannerisms personified all that one thinks of as a true Southern Gentleman. Snow white hair and brilliant blue eyes, set against a summer tan on a ram-rod straight five-foot ten-inch slender frame made for quite an impression. Especially for his greatest admirer, Lucy Mae, his wife of fifty-five years and the mother of their three children. Many who knew them felt theirs was a love story that could be a Southern romantic novel.

Once a world traveler, Jennings' advancing age and declining health now meant he seldom ventured away from Bowling Green, Kentucky, where he lived and worked. He was the patriarch of one of the South's most successful multi-generation, family-owned enterprises, with companies in a variety of industries in several southern states. While not a family member, Ben was one of the company's senior executives and, as Jennings had told him, and others, his most trusted financial advisor.

"Ben," Jennings continued, "I'm helping the founder of Adelaide Holdings. Are you familiar with Adelaide?"

"Since Marla was born there, I know it's a coastal town in Australia west of Melbourne. I didn't know we were involved with any international companies."

"We're not. Adelaide is the name of a holding company located in Kentucky. The founder chose the name just because of the way it sounded."

When Jennings clarified by giving the company's public name, Ben made the connection.

"They're in manufacturing, aren't they? Cosmetics mainly, and other things."

"Correct."

Jennings went on to describe the privately-held company as one of the South's largest manufacturers of environmentally-sensitive cleaning products, as well as the country's premier maker of cosmetics for African-American women.

"How are you involved?" Ben asked.

"Estate-planning for the founder that will coincide with divesture of ownership."

Jennings could easily say in one short sentence what it would take others a paragraph to convey. It was an ability Ben's father also possessed, and one Ben envied. Jennings wasn't just Ben's employer and someone he admired. Despite Ben's age and years of "big city" corporate experience, he regarded the older man as his mentor.

Jennings was also Ben's father's best friend since they were young boys, and together they helped rebuild Ben's life after he lost everything, materially and spiritually, in the Great Recession that began in late 2008. It was Ben's father who re-introduced him to Jennings, and it was the resulting job offer that gave Ben a much-needed lifeline and brought him back to Bowling Green from Chicago five years ago.

"How will the divesture happen? Outright sale? Or maybe a public offering?"

"Neither. The lawyers are creating an Employee Stock Ownership Plan. There'll be a leveraged buy-out by the employees." Jennings continued to explain that if it had been an outright sale, his rough, back-of-the-envelope estimate was that the company's founder and sole shareholder, Jo Gilpin, would have netted over two hundred and fifty million dollars. After taxes."

"Big number," Ben said, stating the obvious. "Have I ever met Joe Gilpin?"

"I don't think so. Certainly not through me."

"So, are you telling me this because you need my help with Mr. Gilpin?"

Ben noticed a smile forming on Jennings' face, something Ben knew almost always foretold an interesting story. If not immediately, then eventually.

"Ben, Gilpin has been funding programs for years to benefit disadvantaged children in Kentucky. I thought the Lauren Minor Taylor Foundation might be a natural fit."

The mention of his late wife's name instantly brought back painful memories. Lauren hadn't survived a stroke when she was only thirty-five. She had successfully beaten cervical cancer earlier, which meant she and Ben couldn't have children. In her memory, Ben had created a foundation to benefit under-privileged children, funded with every dollar of the significant on-going flow of royalties from the popular children's books that had made her a household name.

Ben realized Jennings was looking at him, waiting for his reaction. Embarrassed, Ben asked him to repeat what he'd just said.

Hearing again about Gilpin's potential interest in Lauren's foundation, especially given the amount of money Jennings had mentioned, Ben made no attempt to hide his enthusiasm. "That would be wonderful! If it happens, of course. What should I do?"

"Call Beverly and ask her to join us," Jennings said, gesturing to the phone on the desk. A few minutes later, Beverly Wingate arrived, shorthand pad in hand. She'd been Jennings' administrative assistant for over forty years.

Beverly wore a flowery summer dress appropriate for a conservative office environment. Despite her beautifully styled gray hair, upon first meeting her, no one would believe she was almost seventy and a grandmother of six. The years had been exceedingly kind to her, and Beverly had assisted with a lifetime commitment to health and fitness. Her husband Jesse hadn't shared that commitment, and no one enjoyed the region's comfort food and world-renowned bourbon more than he. Beverly had been a widow for seven years.

Jennings politely gestured for Beverly to take a guest chair in front of Ben's desk, then settled into the matching one next to her. Ben's office was on the top floor of a restored three-story historic building on the town square. When Ben's wife Marla first saw it, she described the décor as "elegantly appointed" with antique Southern furniture and oil paintings of landscapes and horses. Ben changed nothing when Jennings hired him – it was perfect just the way it was, from the vaulted ceilings, to the exposed brick walls and floor-to-ceiling windows, down to the beautiful red and gold wool carpet resting on polished nineteenth century hard-wood floors.

"Beverly, Jo Gilpin is expecting to hear from us. Please send one of those email things and introduce Ben so they can arrange a meeting. I don't need to be involved."

That was a real departure for Jennings, Ben thought. Normally, he would have just picked up the phone since, to Ben's knowledge, he'd never used email himself. When Ben first mentioned getting something online soon after joining the company in the summer of 2009, Jennings jokingly asked if there was a fish at the other end.

Jennings asked Beverly to assist with a few other matters pertaining to Adelaide Holdings before she departed. Her desk was outside Jennings' office at the opposite end of the long hallway lined with more Southern-themed paintings. In Ben's former business life, the décor of offices in Chicago were often indistinguishable from those in Miami, New York or Los Angeles. No such confusion about where in the country he now resided. Ben felt his Bowling Green office was infinitely preferable to the one he had at Lehman Brothers in Chicago. As was his life now, compared to those years that seemed so long ago.

Later in the day, BTaylor@ and JGilpin@ exchanged brief emails, and they agreed to meet the next morning at the company's headquarters in Versailles, near Lexington. Unlike the city in France, in Kentucky it's pronounced ver-SALES.

That evening, over dinner, Ben replayed for Marla the afternoon conversation with Jennings, and told her of the next day's trip. After helping her clear the table, he withdrew to their shared home office and began Internet research on Adelaide Holdings. Ben was surprised to find its web site listed several executive profiles, but no mention of a founder, chairman or CEO. And there was nothing in the site's press section about Gilpin.

Even though the company was private, the Internet opened doors to all kinds of research on virtually anyone and anything. Still, Ben couldn't find a single item on a Joseph Gilpin in connection with the company, or anyone prominent by that name living in the Versailles area. He kept trying to dig deeper, but his sleuthing came to an end when his month-old daughter Danielle awakened crying loudly. It was his turn at late-night parenting, so he tended to her needs by changing her and rocking her back to sleep with her last bottle of the evening.

Looking down at the angelic face of their daughter, who came as a complete surprise to her parents given their ages, a persistent memory entered Ben's mind – his obsession with having a son. An obsession that caused so much pain for him, but even worse, for others who loved him. It wasn't that he didn't have a son. He did. But he'd never seen him, and most likely, never would. Ben shook off the sorrow that always accompanied these thoughts, and abandoned his research. It was late. He fell asleep knowing all would become clearer in a matter of hours.

Marla and Ben tried to follow Beverly's health and fitness example, and that of Ben's father, so breakfast for him the next morning was Greek yogurt and walnuts, chased with a protein drink. After kissing both Marla and Danielle good-bye, he took the elevator down to the enclosed garage on the ground level with a travel mug of coffee in one hand, briefcase in the other. Less than ten minutes later, he'd driven the distance from their downtown home to the on-ramp of I-65 North.

Versailles is about a hundred fifty miles from Bowling Green, mostly interstate, so it took him two and a half hours to reach his destination. As he approached the address he'd been given, he saw a large manufacturing facility sprawling over several acres behind a five-story office building he guessed to be about fifty-thousand square feet. Both buildings, and the tree-lined open areas separating and surrounding them, were as carefully maintained and landscaped as if they were home to an expensive private college.

He parked in one of the spaces designated for guests, locked his silver Lexus hybrid sedan, and checked his reflection in the driver's side window – blue suit, white shirt, muted tie. He gave a slight nervous adjustment to the tie's knot, picked up his black leather Ghurka briefcase, and walked toward the main entrance of a striking red brick and white stone colonial-styled building.

The centerpiece of the lobby caught his eye – an impressive round rug about twelve feet in diameter. He was told later the company's owner selected blue and gold to be consistent with the official colors of the state. For a company headquarters of its size, Ben thought it was odd there were only two chairs in the reception area to accommodate visitors. He then noticed there were no other guests waiting mid-morning on a week day.

He approached the receptionist, who was dressed in a manner befitting a company executive, even though she couldn't have been much more than twenty-five. He handed her his business card and told her he was twenty minutes early for an appointment with Joe Gilpin. She welcomed him, telling him her name was Mary Ann. After quietly calling someone to announce his arrival, she offered him a choice of coffee or bottled water. He declined both and selected one of the two maroon leather guest chairs.

Between the switchboard calls Mary Ann answered, Ben shared his surprise at the limited seating.

"Oh, that's because our owner insists that none of our guests are kept waiting." With a smile, she added, "Even when they're early."

Since he *was* early, Ben looked for a magazine or newspaper to occupy himself. There were none. He realized they would be counter to the "don't keep our guests waiting" culture.

A few minutes later, a tall, slender, strikingly beautiful and impeccably dressed African-American woman entered the lobby. As she walked toward him, Ben guessed she was in her early to mid-forties. He assumed she was Joe Gilpin's personal assistant sent to greet and fetch him.

"Good morning, Ben. I'm Josephine Gilpin. Please call me *Jo*. Thank you for coming."

2

"You look surprised, Ben."

"I am," he admitted, knowing it probably showed on his face and in his demeanor.

Jo had escorted Ben to a modest first-floor interior office located about halfway between the reception area and the windows at the far end of the building. The hallway wall of the office was entirely glass, affording no visual privacy. With no executive desk and chair, the furniture and its arrangement conveyed the look and feel of a residential parlor or living room. It was not a conference room, and not like any executive office he'd ever seen, so Ben concluded their meeting didn't rise to the level of a discussion in the CEO's corner office.

His host motioned for him to sit on the small sofa and, sitting in one of two facing chairs, she began pouring coffee from the carafe on the table between them. Looking around, it slowly dawned on Ben that this might actually *be* her office.

Ben decided to break his self-imposed nutrition rules and accepted Jo's offer of enticing breakfast scones on the tray next to the carafe. His selection was one with caramel icing and, when asked, he answered that he took his coffee as brewed. He sat upright at the edge of the sofa as the cup and saucer were handed to him. He'd never been in such a business setting before, and his discomfort was obvious as his host poured coffee for herself. Like her guest, she didn't add cream or sugar.

"Ben, let me begin with a confession, and then an apology. I'm certain you were expecting *Mr.* Gilpin. Or Joe, with an 'e'. And I went along with the ruse. I apologize for surprising you, maybe even embarrassing you."

"Well, I was surprised, but I wasn't embarrassed." He *was* embarrassed, but wasn't going to admit it.

"I'm glad. Jennings delights in playing this trick on unsuspecting victims, and I've been a reluctant co-conspirator. Most of his other victims over the years have threatened some form of payback, but I doubt any ever followed through."

"That was my first thought," Ben said, relaxing a bit as he thought back to Jennings' use of email for the introduction, which cleverly enabled the surprise.

"I hope you'll look back on this moment with great fondness, and share it with others as part of the lore of Jennings Eldridge."

He nodded and added, "Although I may have unique standing with him to contemplate a get-even of some kind."

"I think we'll both put that in the highly unlikely category. Ben, is there something else?"

"Please forgive my asking, but is this your office?"

Not only was it small without any exterior windows, it didn't have the "I love me" wall usually found in CEO offices where diplomas, bestowed honors and pictures of the executive with celebrities were framed and prominently displayed. Ben knew there was almost always a direct correlation between such mementos and substantial financial contributions, so he was seldom impressed. But in this instance, his curiosity got the better of him.

Jo finished a long sip of coffee, and said, "Yes, this is my office. My guess is you were expecting one many times larger, in a corner, with windows offering the best outside view the building has to offer." Embarrassed once again, Ben could only nod in reply. "I understand that's what everyone expects, but it's something I never aspired to. I've never been a corner-office gal, so to speak. I've always wanted to be in the thick of things, to have my office as close as possible to the people responsible for our success. And I want to be accessible to them without barriers."

"Is that why you don't have a desk?"

"Yes. It can be dysfunctional, at times, but I believe not having one removes an impediment to communication. And I've never had a door."

There was no way he couldn't look, and sure enough, no door to her office. Not that it was just standing open. It wasn't there.

"That certainly gives new meaning to an *open-door policy*," he said, thinking about how this compared to most executives merely saying the words. "Do your other executives have doors to their offices?"

"They don't have offices. They have cubicles. We believe it enhances communication by not creating physical statements of position or authority. And allows everyone to see the outdoors while working indoors."

"Do any of your employees work remotely, say from home?"

"Yes, and it's always the employees' choice if their work makes that feasible. But we ask them to act at home as if they were here."

"No working in pajamas?"

Laughing, Jo replied, "No, we don't care about that. What we *do* care about is an appropriate work-life balance. End their work day at home just as if they were walking out the door here. Don't answer emails or phone calls after hours. It can all wait until the next day."

Ben took it all in, assuming Jo had patiently given these explanations countless times before.

"Different, I know. Ben, I'm not saying what we do here, the business practices we embrace, will work everywhere. But you've seen our financials. I'll put our results, the quality of our service to both our employees and our customers, up against anyone. In any industry."

Instead of correcting her that he hadn't seen her company's financial information, he asked, "What do you mean by service to our employees?"

"Let's leave that for another, and longer, conversation, if you want. Let me just say our management team is deeply committed to servant leadership. It has a Biblical foundation. I'm paraphrasing here, but it says greatness is not measured by the number of servants you have, rather the number of people you serve."

"It's obviously working for you, and your company. I just haven't heard of it before."

"Oh, I think you have. Perhaps it was just stated differently. You know, something like 'Take care of your employees, and they'll take care of your customers.' We didn't invent it. We discovered it. And we work hard every day to be the best at it we can be."

While Ben was thinking that what he'd just heard might be book-worthy, or perhaps a *Harvard Business Review* article, he saw there was *one* framed certificate on display. Her Kentucky Colonel commission. She noticed him looking, and when their eyes once again met, she asked, "Does it represent a common bond between us?"

"It does," he answered, "although I have no idea where my certificate is. Or if I even still have it."

"My appointment was back in the '80s," she said, "when Martha Layne Collins was Kentucky's only-ever woman governor. Now that we Colonels have a woman as our commanding general, and a woman as executive director, I felt moved to display mine. Changing times. And good ones, don't you think?"

"I do. By the way, my wife's full name is Marla Jo – same spelling as yours."

"What a lovely coincidence," Jo said, with warmth in both her voice and her expression. A few seconds of silence signaled a transition from getting acquainted to getting down to business. Or so he thought.

"Ben, I like to begin meetings like this by asking my guests to tell me their story. Will you be so kind as to tell me yours?"

In his twenty-five years in business, especially the two decades in the upper reaches of the country's financial sector, he'd never had a meeting begin this way. The request was as disarming as Jo was charming, and he didn't think to ask what she might already know from Jennings.

"Okay, where would you like me to start?" he asked, feeling sufficiently relaxed to sit a little farther back on the sofa.

"Wherever you like. It's your story."

"I don't remember my birth," he replied, in an effort to be clever while gathering his thoughts, "but it occurred while my father was in law school at the University of Virginia. He and my mother moved back to his home town when he graduated. My mother died when she was young, and my father never remarried."

If people in Kentucky made the name connection with Ben's well-known father, that was fine with him. But he was never the first to mention it.

"After graduating from Western (Ben knew she would know that was Western Kentucky University), I went to Chicago and worked in the financial markets for many years. I was president of a Lehman Brothers subsidiary there when the company imploded at the beginning of the Recession."

"Pardon the interruption," Jo said, "but do you know Christine Lagarde?"

"I know who she is. She's the current head of the International Monetary Fund. Before that, I think she was a lawyer. Why?"

"As a business woman, I pay close attention to what prominent women say. And do. Back in 2008, at the beginning of the recession, she was widely quoted as saying that if Lehman Brothers had been

Lehman Sisters, things would have been very different. Sorry, Ben, I couldn't resist."

"Having been there, been a part of it, lived through it, I can't say I disagree," he said, returning her infectious smile.

"What then?" Jo asked, setting her cup and saucer back on the table. It was then Ben noticed the absence of a wedding ring. Or any rings. Her only jewelry was a simple gold cross on a thin necklace.

Ben decided not to mention his first wife Carol, who was pregnant with their first child when she was killed in a traffic accident in Chicago. But it was what began his downward spiral years ago.

"Tough times," he continued. "Actually, really tough times. But all of my own making. I was highly leveraged, and lost everything. Financially and personally. Honestly, I was in rather desperate straits. But thankfully, two close friends in Chicago stepped in to help, and got me back on track."

"And that track led to Bowling Green?"

"It did. My father and Jennings are old friends, and Dad arranged a job interview that led to my position with Jennings' company."

Jo looked away, and Ben sensed she was now gathering *her* thoughts. When she looked back, she said, "From Jennings I already know quite a bit about the Lauren Miner Taylor Foundation. And about Lauren. Ben, I am so sorry."

This time he took the initiative to pour more coffee, first for Jo, then for himself, to purposely avoid a potentially awkward response, something she sensed. What he didn't know at that moment, but would learn over time, was that her life's challenges had at least been equal to his, though she'd been a much stronger person. A few quiet seconds passed.

"Thank you," she said, as he finished pouring and sat back. "Ben, this is a very big decision for me. The foundation, I mean. And I thought it was important for us to meet, to get to know one another. I hope you're not offended by my questions."

"Not at all. So, a few years after Lauren's death, I married Marla, a professor at Western. We were recently blessed with our first child. A daughter. A surprise, maybe even a bit of a miracle, given our ages."

"That's wonderful! What's her name?"

"Danielle."

"A beautiful name. And a beautiful child, no doubt."

"Well, I'm biased, but Jennings and her grandfather certainly think so. Thankfully, she favors her mother." Hoping for an opportunity for closure, he asked, "Jo, have I given you what want? About me, that is."

"Yes, you have. Thank you."

She *did* say they were meeting to get to know each other, so he took the initiative, and asked, "I know I'm your guest, but would it be impolite for me to ask you to tell me *your* story? I tried to research you yesterday, but I wasn't a match for Jennings' name game."

Jo's acknowledging smile turned to a more serious look when she answered. "Ben, I realize my answer is going to sound unfair, and perhaps even rude, but not today. I get very tired this time of day. But I'd be happy to have some of my story shared with you by others who've known me all my life."

"Jo," he said, hesitating, "I understood Jennings to say you don't have any family."

"That's partially correct. I have no living blood relatives. But there are two who are as close to me as if we were. And they're waiting to speak with you, if you want."

"That's sounds mysterious. How will I find them? And when do you want me to contact them?"

"The *when* would be anytime convenient for Jennings. And your father."

"You know my father?" he asked, completely surprised.

"Ben, your father and Jennings have been in my life since the day I was born. They've been my advisors and mentors, and they remain to this day my dearest friends."

Jennings left *that* out of their pre-meeting meeting, Ben thought, while making certain he'd set up the Joe, not Jo, expectation. He couldn't help wondering what else this journey of discovery had in store for him.

Jo stood, signaling the meeting was ending. As he rose, Ben asked if there was anything else he could tell her, about himself or the foundation.

"Nothing occurs to me now," she answered. "You have my promise I'll carefully consider your foundation in my future planning, and give you an answer very soon." After pausing for a brief moment, she added as she extended her hand, "It was a genuine pleasure meeting you."

The salesman in Ben kicked in, wanting this to not be their only meeting. "I enjoyed meeting you, as well. Perhaps the next time, Marla can come with me. I'd like for you to meet her."

"Ben, I'd love to meet with you, and Marla, but there would be one condition."

Mission accomplished, he told himself. "Of course. Anything. What would we need to do?"

"Bring Danielle with you."

He smiled as much at the thought of his baby daughter as Jo's request. As he was escorted back down the hallway to the lobby, he asked the "next steps" question he was certain she was expecting.

"You can anticipate my decision very soon," was her reply.

From decades of experience, Ben considered himself astute at reading body language, as well as interpreting voice tone and inflection, to give him an indication of probable outcomes. With Jo Gilpin, he gleaned nothing of the sort. She smiled warmly as she shook his hand and thanked him yet again for coming. And she remained in the lobby until he departed, a gesture that meant she didn't once turn her back on her guest.

As he pulled out onto the Blue Grass Parkway to begin the drive back to Bowling Green, he began reflecting on his brief time with this intriguing woman. He was struck by many things, but one in particular was confusing. He placed a call, using the voice-activated dialing feature on his Bluetooth-enabled cell phone.

He wanted answers, and Jo had told him where he could get them.

3

Jo returned to her office and, sitting on the sofa, poured a final cup of morning coffee. She usually arrived at her office before eight when she wasn't traveling, and her tightly-scheduled days were taken up with meetings with both executives and staff, conference calls with current and prospective customers, and the myriad of other activities usually found only in the in-box of the company's CEO. There was no executive dining room, and Jo made it a point to have an unhurried lunch every day among her employees in the company-subsidized cafeteria. She usually called for her driver around six for the half-hour drive to her home in Bardstown, and often worked for a couple of hours before going to bed.

Jo's practice was to clear her emails only twice each day – at ten and at four. She found this discipline enabled her to keep from disrupting the day she'd already planned, and to prepare for the next. The meeting with Ben had delayed her this morning, and when finished, she relaxed and reflected on Jennings Eldridge, the catalyst for the meeting, and on her life's journey – because one would not have been possible without the other.

She often wondered, and lately with increasing frequency, if there *was* such a thing as a normal childhood? The time and place for hers was the largely segregated South of the early 1960's. And she knew her family life would never fit anyone's definition of "normal."

Jo had been inquisitive from a very early age, constantly asking questions about her mother's upbringing and often being distressed by the candid answers she was given. Cynthia Dara Gilpin had been an orphan, passed around from one family member to another. Even though she was very intelligent, Cynthia couldn't afford an education beyond high school. But Jo became excited when her mother told her that after a series of menial jobs in her home town in Mississippi, she was inspired by, and drawn to, the Civil Rights Movement. Still in her late teens, Cynthia became active in the non-violent movement led by Dr. Martin Luther King, a prominent Southern Baptist minister who eventually won the Nobel Peace Prize.

Jo often recalled with a sense of pride that her father, who she'd never met, was a Freedom Rider. He had traveled with brave men and women, black and white, young and old, from northern cities to join organized acts of civil disobedience in an attempt to end segregation of southern bus terminals involved in interstate commerce. On May 20, 1961, her mother and father, two young idealists who were both only eighteen at the time, met at a rally at a church in Montgomery, Alabama.

Later that evening, they became intimate, swept up in the energy of The Movement. Jo's mother saw no future in that one-time passionate coupling, and didn't ask for his address or phone number. All she knew was that he was from Detroit, and that he returned to his New England college campus on a bus late the next day.

When Jo became an adult, she pieced together bits of information and learned her father's identity. Like her, and her mother, he was an only child. He had accepted a three-year army commitment in order to finance his college education, but died in combat in Vietnam in 1966, just three months shy of fulfilling that obligation.

Despite Jo's assurances to the contrary, her mother felt deeply embarrassed about the circumstances of Jo's conception, as well as the fact Jo grew up in a home without a father. Jo longed to tell her mother what she'd learned about her father, but was so uncertain about her mother's reaction she decided against it. She also thought about contacting her father's parents, but concluded she couldn't do that and not tell her mother. So she kept quiet. But each time she traveled to Washington, D.C., she visited the Vietnam War Memorial, and she cherished the pencil tracing of his name she'd made on her first visit.

While pregnant, Cynthia gathered her courage and took a bus from Alabama to Bowling Green, Kentucky, the home of two of the young white Freedom Riders who'd been especially kind to her. She remembered their names and home town, but knew nothing else except that they'd looked and sounded prosperous. With no one else to turn to, she hoped one of them could give her a job, any job, or help her find one.

One of the men, Jennings Eldridge, turned out to be the son of a successful businessman, and Cynthia was offered a kitchen job in one of their restaurants. And when Jo was born, her mother was surprised to learn the hospital expenses were anonymously paid in full, although she was certain she knew the identity of her benefactor. When she was able to return to work, a job at a nursing home also owned by the Eldridge family allowed her to bring the baby with her. Jo's mother delighted in telling her more than once over the years what a source of amusement and entertainment Jo was for the residents until she was old enough to begin school.

With only a high school diploma and a small child to care for, Cynthia struggled, but was always able to provide for the two of them. Despite her limited formal education, Cynthia encouraged her daughter in her studies, and helped when it was needed. Because of her mother, Jo developed a lifelong love of learning, and excelled academically. Just as her mother could have, had circumstances been different.

When Jo was nine years old, she saw a replay on television of the *I Have a Dream* speech delivered by Dr. King on the steps of the Lincoln Memorial on August 28, 1963. She was so mesmerized that at first she didn't see her mother watching her from the doorway. Then she heard her crying softly. When Jo turned in her direction, her mother wiped her tears and sat silently on the floor next to her daughter, holding her hand. Jo came to realize the tears were because of many things. Because her mother had *been* there. Because she actually *knew* him. Because of what could have been for Cynthia, if it hadn't been for the pregnancy. But Jo recalled her mother never expressed any regrets, only unselfish and unconditional love for her daughter.

That evening, at dinner, Jo told her mother how much seeing that speech had inspired her. For the first time, Cynthia told her daughter details of her brief involvement in the Civil Rights Movement, and showed her the only picture she had of Jo's father. There he was, with Cynthia, standing alongside the man who gave that inspired speech.

About a week later, Jo came home from school and found a package on the kitchen table, with a note that simply said, *To Mary, From Jennings*. (Deeply religious, her mother had named her only child Mary Josephine after Mary and Joseph, but it wasn't until after Jo graduated from college that she began going by Josephine.) Her mother had mentioned to Jennings that Jo had been inspired by the speech, and he saw to it something special happened for the little girl of one of his father's employees.

When Jo unwrapped it, she discovered a tape player and a recording of the speech. She played it over and over until she'd memorized it, then recited it in her mind until she fell asleep each night after saying her prayers. Jo became fixated on dreams, and their realization. One evening, as Jo and her mother sat side by side on the sofa in the living room of their small, two-bedroom home, she asked her mother if it was wrong for her to be so consumed with dreaming about her future, especially since she would have to travel so far to fulfill her dreams.

Cynthia took both of Jo's hands in hers, and with tears brimming in her eyes, said, "Honey, dreams never come true for those who never dream. You must follow yours, wherever they take you."

And Jo did.

4

"Mysterious, I'll grant you," Marla said, setting her wine glass down. Ben had just finished telling her about his Versailles meeting as they were having dinner that same evening.

Their home on Park Row occupied the entire top floor of an historic building Ben and his father had converted on the street across the town square from the building that housed the Main Street offices of Ben's employer. All buildings on The Square abutted each other and none exceeded three stories.

Marla listened intently, thinking to herself how handsome her husband was. He was approaching his fifty-fifth birthday, what he called "the double nickel," but most people would guess him to be much younger. He was six-one, same as his father, but with brown eyes instead of blue. He carried his 190 pounds in a manner reflecting his commitment to working out with a Pilate's trainer several times a week. Topping it off, literally, was a full head of beautiful brown hair that was graying ever so slightly.

"Jo certainly sounds like an interesting woman," Marla added. "What's got me really curious is the connection to your father and Jennings. Must be a real story there."

"I'm having lunch with both of them tomorrow," Ben said, "so I know what you and I'll be talking about over dinner tomorrow night."

"I can't wait. Do you think she'll become involved with the foundation?"

"I was thinking about that on the drive home – how we never got around to discussing the purpose of our meeting."

"Perhaps *her* purpose was only to get to know you. She may have already learned all she needed to know about the foundation from Jennings."

"She did say something about getting to know each other. So you think it was just personal, not business?"

"Ben, where women and business are concerned, *personal* counts – often as much, or more, than what men may value. If she doesn't like you, and respect you, then I doubt the foundation's mission statement or balance sheet will matter."

Ben then recounted Jo's *Lehman Sister's* comment.

"See?" When he didn't respond, she changed the subject, and asked, "How are things at the office?"

"The succession planning is rather overwhelming," Ben said, "but we're getting our arms around it. Jennings has been all-in, given he knows it all centers around preparing for what happens after he dies."

Ben preferred to leave work behind at the office, usually only talking in generalities about where he spent most of his weekday waking hours. What he *had* shared with Marla recently was that his focus had been almost entirely on helping Jennings facilitate leadership succession of his far-flung, privately-held business empire soon to enter a virtually unheard-of fourth generation of family ownership and management. He told her Jennings had agreed to electronic cataloging and storage of voluminous records and documents accumulated over almost six decades in business.

"Something interesting happened a few days ago," Ben continued, "and I'd like to get your opinion."

Marla had begun clearing the dinner dishes from the table, but she sat back down, saying, "Always happy to give my opinion. Are we talking personal or professional?"

"Actually, it involves *your* profession. And my new-found passion. Besides you, of course."

"Interesting. And do you have your passions properly prioritized?"

"Nice alliteration," Ben acknowledged. "You first, of course. And Danielle. Work. And then my desire to continue writing. Anonymously, that is."

"Well said. Now, back to my opinion. What's up?"

"In cataloging Jennings' private papers, one of the lawyers found a box containing a collection of personal journals. I told her to put them in my office, and when I looked in the box a few hours later, I found two neatly organized rows of notebooks of various sizes and colors, each held together with a rubber band. Tempted as I was, I decided to leave them untouched."

"And?"

"When I asked Jennings later that afternoon, he explained his habit of writing down the thoughts and phrases of others he heard or read that were impactful to him at the time. Over the decades, he would constantly re-read those notebooks. 'Going back to the well' he called it. He'd never mentioned them before, and I've been working closely with him for several years. Impulse got the better of me, and I asked if I could read them. I immediately regretted asking, but he told me to go ahead."

"And have you read them?" Marla asked, refilling her wine glass and gesturing invitingly with the bottle. He declined by placing his hand over his glass, and continued.

"Not all of them. I haven't had time. But that's what I wanted to talk to you about. I think some, actually most, of the material in the journals could be converted into an inspirational book that could make an impact on the lives of others. Honestly, Marla, I was moved by what I read, and I think it would be a shame for this material not to be shared."

"Have you talked to Jennings? And by the way, I saw that."

"Saw what?" Ben asked, trying and failing at achieving innocence in either his voice or expression.

"Slipping her scraps from the table. Ben, we had an understanding. If you keep that up, Madison will set a weight record for Cavalier King Charles spaniels."

"Okay," he said, looking down at the dog at his feet. "Sorry girl." He patted her on the head, and continued. "Yes, I talked with Jennings. He said it's not something he's ever contemplated. And he doesn't share my enthusiasm for a book. Not at all."

"Did he tell you why?"

"Although he complimented me for the idea, and said the journals served him well, he doesn't want any publicity for himself. What I think *did* catch his attention was the idea of helping others."

"All that makes Jennings, well, Jennings," Marla offered. "So, despite his reaction, are you going to pursue it with him?" When Ben nodded, she added, "How do you see a book like this coming together?"

"Not certain. I have lots of thoughts about how to approach it, but I need my thinking much more advanced before talking with him again."

"That's smart. Now, if it happens, do you see yourself as the author?"

"Yes," Ben answered, hesitantly, sensing where Marla was going. "And Jennings would insist upon it."

"Then what about the sequel you've been planning?" Ben had already invested substantial time, with Marla's assistance, outlining a sequel to his novel, *Southern Longings.*

"Given Jennings' age, if he agreed, mine would simply have to wait."

Ben and Marla had met three years earlier when he was referred to her for help with his debut novel. She'd published three books of her own, and her university teaching position allowed her the freedom to freelance as a professional writing coach and editor. She had a stable of successful author clients who had provided a constant flow of referrals, but her dream to be a successful author had thus far eluded her. Her books went virtually unnoticed while Ben's became a bestseller.

"You're *that* passionate about this journals-to-book project?" Marla asked.

"Yes, almost more than I can describe."

"All right, what else?" she asked, taking her last sip of wine.

"We know Jennings doesn't want to be identified in any way with the book, and since I work for him, me as the author would compromise that."

"Looking for ideas?"

"Anything. Everything."

"Well, without seeing the journals, or having any idea what you're thinking, why not write it in the voice of a fictionalized character, which protects Jennings' identity? And repeat what you did with your own book. Use a *nom de plume*."

Looking relieved, Ben asked, "Marla, does it ever trouble you to point out the painfully obvious to me in my times of need?"

"Not so far, and likely not in the future," she answered, with a mischievous grin beginning to light up her face. "And in repayment, how about you taking Danielle duty for the rest of the evening?"

"How about an IOU? You know the Cubs are on TV tonight."

"No time like the present to introduce our daughter to America's pastime."

They had just begun clearing the dishes when, with a smile and a tilt of her head in the direction of the cries of the newest Cubs fan, Marla said, "Game time!"

As she finished the kitchen chores, Marla reflected on their dinner conversation. She could tell Ben was enthralled with his idea, but she knew his enthusiasm would soon give way to the realization his days were already fully consumed with his duties at the company, and his evenings and weekends as a husband and father. But in just his brief description, she saw a possible extension of his idea that would be *her* idea. And involve her.

Before falling asleep, Marla had wistful thoughts, remembering what it was like for her not so long ago to also have interesting meetings, away from home – and with adults. She loved her life as a new mother, but was struggling with feelings of envy for all Ben had going in is life. She regretted that hers had narrowed so dramatically in the year since she became pregnant.

She was determined things would change. And soon.

5

Ben's father was seated next to Jennings when Ben joined them for lunch the next day. Both men, now in their late seventies, had the same coloring of hair, eyes and complexion, as well as similarity of features. Although Ben's father was two inches taller, they could easily be mistaken for brothers.

"Good morning, Ben. Did you enjoy your first meeting with *Mr.* Gilpin?" Jennings asked.

"Yes, sir, I enjoyed meeting Josephine Gilpin immensely. And I was as surprised as you would have anticipated. But then again, it wasn't a first for you, was it?"

Both older men smiled broadly, exchanging knowing glances. They were impeccably dressed in summer-weight suits, Ben's father in light grey with a traditional dark blue tie, and Jennings in tan seer-sucker with a solid brown bow tie. Both had a white silk handkerchief peeking out of the breast pocket of their jackets.

Marla had assured Ben more than once that these men could still cause fluttering hearts among women in town of a certain age. If true, Ben knew they would respond appropriately, and appreciatively, as the true Southern Gentlemen they were.

"No, it wasn't," Jennings answered. "As I'm sure Jo shared with you. She's gracefully indulged these introductions, although they've become increasingly less frequent in recent years."

Ben thought Jennings' use of the term "graceful" in describing her was spot on. It was one of the many positive impressions he'd taken away from his brief meeting.

"Ben, before we go any further, let me congratulate you again on your book." This time it was his father speaking. "I saw in yesterday's paper it's still on the New York Times best-seller list. And it's been there for several weeks, right?"

"Yes, sir. Twelve to be exact, but then who's counting?" he replied, trying to appear modest but unable to suppress a grin.

Southern Longings was released at the end of 2015, and had been gaining traction month after month. At that moment, Ben thought of Lauren, and how proud she would have been. Marla and Lauren had actually met a few times, but it was before he began his novel. Since his writing had brought Marla into his life a couple of years after Lauren died, there was a literary thread connecting his past and his present. And, hopefully he thought, his future.

"And who besides a few of us even knows. Right?" Jennings added.

"That would be true," Ben answered.

"Do you have any regrets about using the pen name?" Jennings asked. "I mean, almost no one knows it's you who wrote a best-selling book. Something very few people ever accomplish."

"Not for a single moment," Ben replied. "I saw how much Lauren struggled with her notoriety."

He couldn't forget how Lauren had longed for an impossible return to anonymity and privacy. He had no way of knowing if his book would be successful, of course, but he knew he didn't want to have to try to put the genie back in the bottle if what actually did happen, happened.

The waiter brought Ben back to the present. "May I tell you today's specials?"

While his father and Jennings ordered, Ben looked around at the handsome restoration. Occupying the ground level of another historically designated building on The Square, Main Fare was a white table cloth restaurant, open for both lunch and dinner, just a couple of minutes' walk from the office. They were seated at a round four-seat table in a quiet alcove, away from the noise of both the front door and the kitchen entrance in the back.

All three ordered a cup of the day's black bean soup special, and despite the enticing entrée selections, they all opted for the chopped Cobb salad. And sweet tea, of course, although Ben was the only one going for the higher octane version. His dining companions selected *half-and-half* – sweet tea diluted with regular tea that didn't have sugar boiled into it.

They took turns sharing thoughts on the day's local, state and national events until their meals were served, at which time Jennings offered a quiet blessing.

"Jo Gilpin is an interesting woman," Ben said, as they began to eat, "but we didn't really talk about the foundation, and very little about her company. And certainly nothing about her."

"If she ran true to form, she asked you to tell her *your story.* Did she?" Jennings asked.

"Yes. It was a first for me. And a disarming one. When I finished, I asked her to tell me her story, but she said that was to come from the two of you."

"And it will," Jennings said, "but first, tell us about your meeting."

Ben briefly shared impressions of his visit, from the welcome he received, to the uniqueness of Jo's office, to the way she approached their time together. And the personal send-off from the company's chief executive. He ended by saying, "Now it's your turn."

"Fair enough. I'll tell you about her business, and your father will tell you about Jo."

Jennings looked at Ben's father, who concurred with a nod, and continued. "Ben, you already know a great deal about Jo and her company because you led the analysis of the SAE Company. Remember?"

So *that's* why Jo thought he'd seen her financials, Ben thought. SAE was a company Jennings had asked him recently to assess in what Ben thought was early-stage due diligence for a potential acquisition. It was Jennings' practice to get Ben's impressions based solely on the numbers, not colored by anecdotal information he could research by knowing the name of the entity. All files needed an internal working name, so Ben had put his college fraternity on it.

With that disclosure, Ben knew SAE Company was not a potential acquisition, rather one in which the sole shareholder intended a leveraged buy-out that rewarded and left in place her loyal executive team. And it would make shareholders of every person employed by the company at the time of the ownership change.

Jennings talked for just a couple of minutes about Jo's business career, painting with broad strokes and few details. Ben's father then took over and, as portions of Mary Josephine Gilpin's story unfolded with his eloquent telling, Ben was in awe. As he listened, he felt a tug, deep down, that her story, like Jennings', needed to be told as an inspiration to others. As his father finished, Ben sensed a missing piece – an incomplete story. Then he remembered the thought he'd had the day before while driving away from her office.

"There *was* something about the meeting with Jo," Ben said.

"What's that, son?"

"I thought it was odd she deferred the telling of her story to the two of you. But also odd because of the additional reason she gave. She said she was tired, and that she got tired at that time of day."

"I'm not certain I understand."

"Dad, it was only late morning. She's a company CEO with a ton of responsibility."

"Ben," Jennings said, choosing his words carefully, "it could be any of a number of things. But the most important thing for us to share with you now is that after your meeting, Jo called me."

"And?" Ben said, literally holding his breath.

"She's decided to bequeath one-fourth of her estate to Lauren's foundation."

Ben's quick mental calculation made his mouth go dry. He reached for his water glass.

"Now," Jennings said, folding his napkin and placing it on the table, "because of the ESOP structure, the money will be paid to the foundation over time, much like Lauren's book royalties. But still, sixty to seventy million dollars, give or take, was a worthy investment of your time yesterday, don't you think?"

"I don't know what to say. And we all know the sale had been made by the two of you before I went to Versailles. Am I right?"

"Well," Jennings allowed, "we may have helped the cause a little bit."

"A *little* bit? I think what's much closer to the truth is that the two of you had the deal signed, sealed and delivered. All I had to do was not screw it up with a bad first impression."

Their smiling faces were all the confirmation Ben needed. "Dad, is there any way you can also be involved? Maybe not now, but sometime in the future?"

"Both Jo and Jennings have asked me the same thing, and my answer may surprise you. Yes."

For decades, Benjamin Taylor, Sr., had been highly visible, locally and in Frankfort, the state capital. And, on rare occasions, the national stage. Throughout his career, his reputation was unblemished and his integrity above reproach. Others in town, close friends and casual acquaintances alike, affectionately and respectfully referred to him as The Judge when talking *about* him, and Judge when speaking *to* him.

"I've been waiting for a time when the three of us were together," he said, touching his napkin to the edge of his mouth before returning it to his lap, "to tell you I'm going to announce I won't be standing for re-election in November. I'll be fully retired by the end of January."

Ben's silence, and his expression, conveyed his surprise. He'd wanted, hoped for, for years that his father would make that decision, but never let himself anticipate when it would happen. As the Chief Justice of the Kentucky Supreme Court, Benjamin Taylor, Sr. was revered by the other justices, and most of the attorneys who appeared before him. He loved the law, and he did great work for the people of Kentucky.

"Dad, I'm delighted," Ben finally said. "Marla and I've been hoping to spend more time with you, especially as Danielle grows older. Jennings, are you surprised?"

"I suspected, but didn't know until just now," Jennings answered, discretely looking at his wrist watch. "And like you, I'm pleased for your father. For all of us, actually."

Ben had learned his first time at Main Fare with Jennings that no check would be presented. Everyone was his guest, and the bill would be sent directly to Beverly for payment at the end of the month. But Jennings would always seek out the waiter and discretely give him or her at least a twenty percent gratuity so they wouldn't have to wait.

Jennings said there was another matter he needed to discuss with The Judge, so they all agreed to meet again at five in Jennings' office for a celebratory tasting of bourbon from his private collection. Walking back to the office, Ben reflected on each topic discussed. Despite all the good news about foundations and retirement, he couldn't shake the nagging feeling there was something left unsaid.

6

It had rained late in the afternoon, so Marla and Ben weren't plagued by pesky insects as they enjoyed their wine and salads on their rooftop deck. Ben had just told Marla about his father's upcoming retirement.

"Ben, that's great! Were you as surprised as I am?"

"I was," Ben answered, "and I honestly think Jennings was, too. At least by the timing. I don't think he knew."

"January's going to come very soon. Did your father say anything about his immediate plans?"

"Only that he's going to assist Jennings as an advisor to Jo's company and a new foundation she's creating."

"What sort of foundation?"

"All they said was it'll fund medical research of some kind in addition to helping at-risk children."

Danielle was sleeping in a small antique cradle Ben's father had given them, positioned next to the teakwood table where they were sitting. As they set aside empty salad bowls and turned their attention to the steaks Ben had prepared on the outdoor grill, Marla asked what else he'd learned in the two meetings.

Ben briefly recounted what he'd been told about Jo's company, and her life.

"Lots of layers," Marla said, "and likely many more. Do you think you'll see her again?"

"Yes. To help with the ESOP implementation, then later with her foundation."

"Seventy million dollars is such a huge amount. When will it go to Lauren's foundation?"

"After Jo dies. It'll come from her estate, and she could easily live for decades. It's possible I won't be around when it happens."

"Don't bet on it. I invested in you for the long term – emphasis on *long*. Anyway, it's an incredibly generous donation whenever it happens, and you were obviously very persuasive."

"Not at all. I found out my father and Jennings had already discussed everything with her in detail. Meeting me yesterday was just a formality."

"I think you're selling yourself short," Marla said, "but then I'm biased, aren't I?" She was warmed by both the setting summer sun and the wine, and by thoughts of how blessed her life was with Ben and their baby. And then an especially warming thought entered her mind.

"You've had quite a day. Danielle *is* sleeping, the dishes can wait, and we don't have many early evening opportunities when neither of us is tired to…." At that moment, Danielle let them know with a loud and persistent cry she was no longer sleeping.

"My turn," Ben said.

"No, I'll take her."

Ben offered to clear the table and bring the cradle when he came down, Marla carefully navigated the stairs leading down into the house. Looking at the now-quiet child in her arms, her mind flashed back several weeks to the maternity ward at Community Hospital.

◆ ◆ ◆

"What?" Marla asked sleepily.

"I know we've talked a lot about other names," Ben said, "but I'd like you to consider naming her Danielle."

"Her" was the day-old baby cradled in her mother's arm. Ben was sitting in a chair next to the bed in a single-occupant hospital room on the maternity floor.

It had been a difficult birth. Marla was tired, and wasn't thinking clearly. So she didn't make the connection. Otherwise, she wouldn't have asked, "Where did *that* come from?"

"Daniel."

Her sudden understanding, combined with emotion and exhaustion, caused her to start crying. Ben handed her the handkerchief he always carried, and when she'd dried her tears, and was able to speak, all she could get out was one word.

"Why?"

"Simple, really. You'll live every day of your life with the memory of Lauren. And her foundation. I want us to also live every day with the memory of Daniel."

Daniel was Marla's first husband, an Australian military pilot killed in a training accident. In an act of heroism, when his plane's engine failed shortly after takeoff, he steered it away from a residential area rather than parachuting out and saving himself. They had no children, her parents were deceased, and she had no siblings. Ben and his father, and now their daughter, were her family.

Given all that had happened in their lives before they met, Ben and Marla felt they'd had more than their fair share of sorrows. A baby coming when she was thirty-seven meant all the more to both of them, and now Ben's naming suggestion felt like such a remarkable expression of love that it left her speechless.

"I know you're really tired, and I've just sprung this on you, so I have a suggestion."

"What?" Marla managed to ask.

"Either say yes, or that you need to think about it. For now, I'm going to leave and let the two of you get some sleep. Actually, just you, since she's doing fine in that department."

◆ ◆ ◆

As she put Danielle in the bassinet along the wall opposite the bed, Marla could hear Ben taking a shower. Sitting down in the rocking chair in the corner, her thoughts turned to their dinner conversation.

Ben had so much going on in his life, yet hers seemed limited to taking care of their daughter, and supporting whatever he was doing. She loved her family, but missed her daily campus routine, surrounded by highly educated adults and mostly motivated students. She couldn't shake feelings of envy, and no matter how hard she tried not to, she was regretting her decision to take a lengthy sabbatical after her maternity leave.

Her downbeat train of thought derailed when her naked husband entered the bedroom. New thoughts, and warm familiar feelings having nothing to do with sun or wine, overtook her. And she could tell he was having the same thoughts.

Their lovemaking was unhurried, and Marla was grateful her husband understood the importance of remaining together afterwards. It was quite some time before he got up from the bed, picked up the hastily discarded towel from the floor, and headed toward the bathroom. But he stopped short of his destination, turned around, and asked if she was up for one more disclosure from his day.

"After what we just experienced, I'm up for anything," Marla answered. "Talking. Not talking. A repeat performance later on. Anything."

Sudden modesty overtook him, and he wrapped the towel around his waist as he returned to sit on the edge of the bed beside her.

"I did have a couple of disappointments among all the good news. Jennings gave me his answer regarding the book. It was no."

"Did he tell you why?"

"He said he'd discussed it with Dad after lunch, and they both think the idea may have merit. But Jennings said not now."

"Why?"

"Several reasons, but basically he doesn't want either of us distracted from the more important business things we're doing. With Dad standing there, and me knowing he agreed with Jennings, I didn't argue my case."

"I'm truly sorry, Ben. I know how excited you were about the project. I know this is a big disappointment, but at the risk of telling you what you already know, it *is* Jennings' company, and they are *his* journals."

"I've had a few hours to think about it, and they're right. My enthusiasm had separated me from reality. All my company responsibilities, as well as with you and Danielle. It's for the best."

"You said he told you not now, and that's not the same as no. Ben, it's possible he might be willing to reconsider later," Marla said, encouragingly.

"I hadn't thought of it that way. You may be right. Anyway, it definitely was a not-now." He leaned forward and kissed her, adding, "Do you want anything? I'm going downstairs for a glass of juice."

"No, honey, but thanks. You've already given me what I wanted. Needed. Wanted *and* needed. You haven't lost your touch. Make that touches. Let's not go so long between times, okay?"

"At your service, ma'am." Ben stood and gave her a loving smile along with a mock salute, a gesture that caused the towel to fall to his ankles. They both laughed so hard they woke Danielle, with Ben agreeing with Marla that laughing was another thing they hadn't done often enough lately.

A half-hour later Ben and Danielle were asleep, but Marla was wide awake, her mind playing with Ben's news, adding it to thoughts she'd been struggling with for weeks. She wasn't ready to say anything yet, but Ben's disappointment held the possibility of an opportunity for her. It would take some careful orchestration with three other people, but she figured she was just the orchestra leader to pull it off.

Before falling asleep, she remembered Ben hadn't shared his second disappointment of the day.

7

"You look very happy," Ben said, grinning as he joined his wife and their daughter in the kitchen the next morning.

"Well, you certainly know how to put a smile on a Southern gal's face."

He was dressed for work in a tailored blue suit, white dress shirt with faint blue stripping, accented with a yellow tie with touches of blue. His brown laced shoes were polished to a high sheen, as they always were.

Mornings usually began for Marla without much thought to fashion, unless she was going somewhere away from home. And that hadn't been very often since Danielle arrived. No plans today meant she was in pale green workout attire – a long-sleeved top and matching shorts that showed off her toned legs. Not having to worry about shoes most mornings was one of the benefits of her current lifestyle, and that morning she was worry-free – at least regarding shoes.

"You do realize I'm over a decade older than you," he said, as he poured coffee for both of them.

"Are you asking me to make allowances for your age, given that I'm what's going to keep you young?"

"It's not that I'm ungrateful. Believe me, I am. Just preparing both of us for that inevitable day when the little blue pill enters our lives."

"Not a problem," Marla answered. "Better living through chemistry, I always say. Scrambled, or over easy?"

"Me or the eggs."

"Down boy."

"Over easy, like me."

Marla looked at her smiling husband and decided there was no time like the present to begin orchestrating her idea. If he didn't warm to it right away, it certainly wouldn't be because he was in a bad mood.

"Ben, I was thinking about what you said last night. About the book. I have an idea, if you have time. Or it can wait until another time."

"Now's as good a time as any. Shoot."

"Well, you have a not-now from Jennings."

"That's true."

"What about Jo Gilpin?"

"I don't follow. What about Jo?"

"Okay, hear me out for a minute. You said Jo told you she's always regarded Jennings as her mentor."

"And my father," Ben interrupted.

"Right, but has your father kept journals?"

"Not that I'm aware of."

"Okay, so Jo said Jennings has always been a mentor to her, which means for a long time. Is it possible she followed his example, and kept journals of her own?" She could tell Ben immediately knew where she was going. But he didn't interrupt. "If she has, maybe *she'd* consider the journals-to-book idea. You told me that after listening to your father and Jennings at lunch, you thought hers was almost as compelling a success story as Jennings'. And in some ways, even more so."

"Gender and ethnicity?" Ben's words could have been a question or a statement, and either way her response was the same.

"Yes."

"Marla, that's brilliant!"

"Thanks. More coffee?" she asked, pushing her chair back.

"No thanks. I'll get more at the office. Okay, when I see Jennings, I'll ask him if his journaling is an activity shared by Jo."

"Then what?" she asked, knowing full well where Ben was headed. But as was often the case, he thought he was leading the parade, with her a respectful two steps behind. Little did he know she was at least that many steps *ahead* of him. As she often was.

"If she does journal, I'll ask Jennings' permission to approach Jo with the idea, since the only way I would know would be from him. If he says yes, I'll call her and go see her."

"Alone?"

"Well, yes. Who else would I take?"

"Me."

"You?"

"I'm the only *me* in the room," Marla said, after jokingly looking around.

"Alright," he said, smiling. "And come to think of it, Jo did ask me to bring you and Danielle to our next meeting."

Ben stood and approached her for what he assumed would be a *Bye honey, I'm off to work* kiss. He stopped when she added, "Not so fast. Assuming you get a yes from both Jennings and Jo, who's going to collaborate with her? Certainly not you."

"And why not?" Ben asked, defensively. He sat back down.

"You just got through telling me yesterday you agreed with Jennings that your company plate was full. And that adding in Danielle and me meant it was spilling over. Other than your enthusiasm once again taking over, what's changed?"

"Well, there is all that," he said, his tone softening. "Anything else?"

"You need more?"

"Let's just say for the purposes of discussion – yes."

"Okay. If you were writing Jennings' book, I understand how you could relate, one businessman to another." He nodded. "But do you really think you'd be able to achieve a truly credible understanding of what women, or more specifically, a woman of color, must accomplish in order to be successful?"

"Successful how?" Ben's voice was growing weaker as hers was growing stronger.

"Pick one. Business. Government. Politics. Higher Education. Athletics. Philanthropy. Military. Whatever."

"Okay, then who would work with her?"

"Me."

"You?"

"I'm still the only me in the room." Internally, she gave herself high fives for orchestrating the conversation toward her desired outcome, and she decided to cut to the chase rather than continue to banter back and forth as they often did. "Ben, I'm saying the possibility that Jo also has journals was *my* idea. I'm saying that if she does, and if she would agree, I'd have the experience, the expertise, and most importantly, the *time* to produce a book with her."

Ben's silence made her think she'd overplayed her hand, coming on too strong, too quickly. And his expression didn't offer any clues. She was about to back-track, regroup and try a different approach later when he spoke. "I agree. Everything you just said makes sense." He glanced at the clock on the kitchen wall. "But I do need to get to the office."

"Thank you for agreeing with me, Ben. But there *is* one thing you can do that I can't."

"What's that?"

"Talk with Jennings. That has to happen before you can say anything to Jo."

"Okay, I'll do it today. Now I really do need to get going."

They kissed at the front door, and as he turned to leave, she gently touched his shoulder. He turned back, and she silently mouthed the words, "Thank you."

"You bet," he said, kissing her again before departing.

After he left, Marla remembered he said he'd had two disappointments in his conversation with Jennings the day before. The "not now" decision on the book was one. What was the other?

Compared to her pre-pregnancy life, Marla's days passed slowly. This day would pass even slower, she thought, waiting for Ben's return home with answers to both questions.

8

Jennings had been resistant when three offices were combined into one for him several years ago, but he'd faced two women determined to make it happen. Beverly Wingate and Lucy Mae Eldridge were of like mind that his office needed to be large enough to tastefully showcase all the business and family memorabilia accumulated over several decades. And with the assistance of a skilled decorator, they were successful. The result was showcase-worthy in either *Architectural Digest* or *Southern Living*, a suggestion Jennings rejected at first mention. So Ben was grateful to be among the relatively few who would ever see it.

Ben guessed the office was at least nine hundred square feet. It had floor-to-ceiling windows on two sides, with exposed brick walls and vaulted ceilings, as well as beautiful antique wool rugs covering portions of the polished 19th century hard-wood floors. Unlike all the other offices, there wasn't a computer anywhere to spoil the period-perfect elegance.

Ben stood in the open office doorway, emulating Jennings' approach to his executives when he respectfully interrupted their work. "Jennings, do you have a moment?"

"Of course. What's on your mind?" he answered, motioning for Ben to occupy one of the guest chairs across from his desk.

"Jo Gilpin. Ever since I met her."

"I'm not surprised. Anything specific?"

"Yes. A question. In our meeting, she told me she's always regarded you has her mentor. I was wondering if perhaps part of that mentoring might have involved encouraging her to keep journals. Just as you have."

"Very perceptive. She does. We've compared entries many times over the years."

Ben sat quietly. Jennings also remained silent. Ben spoke first.

"I'm not trying to re-open a discussion about yours. I just thought that Jo's journals, if she had them, might offer a similar book opportunity, but from a different perspective. You know, a successful woman entrepreneur."

"Ben, what's in mine served me well. My guess is Jo will feel the same way about hers, although if she gives you permission to read them, you'll find diamonds compared to my lumps of coal."

"We'll agree to disagree about that," Ben answered, smiling.

"If Jo agrees to make a book from hers, I still have the same concern about your time."

"I agree. But it's Marla who's offering her time. Truth be known, she would've been much more qualified to collaborate with you. And that goes double if Jo agrees."

Jennings looked at Ben for the longest time. "A word of advice from an old man. What you've just told me about Marla's talent and ability. Make certain you also tell her."

Ben thought about his conversation with Marla, and felt chagrined. "I will."

Back in his office, he realized he hadn't asked permission to tell Jo how he'd learned about her journals. Jennings just gave it implicitly with his "ask her" comment. Ben concluded that was sufficient and looked for Jo's number stored in his cell phone. He dialed, but Jo wasn't available. He left a message with Mary Ann, the receptionist, and as he ended the call, his eyes were drawn to Marla's picture on his desk.

He thought about the first time they met, at her office, to discuss his book. She wasn't what he'd pictured for a university professor, certainly not what he remembered from when he was on the same campus as a student over thirty years earlier. Marla stood a slender five-eight. Naturally curly brown hair and soft green eyes set off a visage that was beautiful even without a touch of make-up. She was truly blessed with both brains and beauty.

His cell phone began vibrating on his desk.

"Good morning, Ben," Jo said, returning his call. "It's nice to hear your voice again. And I want to thank you for taking the time to drive up here to meet with me earlier this week."

"Very kind of you, Jo, but I'm actually calling to express my thanks to *you*, on behalf of the foundation."

"Truthfully, learning you were a fellow Kentucky Colonel was all it took to persuade me."

"I think the real truth is Jennings and my father had done the persuading long before you met me. I'm just grateful I didn't undo their work."

"Colonel Taylor, after meeting you, there wasn't a chance of that happening. Now, what can I do for you today?"

"Jennings asked me to assist with the ESOP transition, so I need to meet with you again. I was calling to ask when would be a good time."

"Let me look at my calendar. How about the day after tomorrow, at ten?"

"That's perfect. I'll only need about an hour."

"Ben, is it possible Marla and the baby could accompany you? I'd love to meet them, but I'll understand if it would be too much trouble."

Ben felt relieved. Her request just eliminated his being the one to bring Marla into the discussion – and to the meeting. He knew Marla would agree it was a good omen. "I know Marla would be delighted, and it will be the first road trip for both of them since Danielle was born."

"Danielle. I remember you told me. What a beautiful name! I can't wait to meet them."

She asked to meet at her home in Bardstown, thirty minutes closer to Bowling Green than her Versailles office. After writing down her address, he said, "Jo, I have an idea to share with you, something I've discussed with Jennings. Has nothing to do with the ESOP or the foundations, just more easily explained, I think, in person. And I didn't want to surprise you."

"Well, that sounds intriguing, but you said the magic word – *Jennings*. Anything he's involved with will be of interest to me. So, yes, of course."

Ben hung up, settled back in his office chair with his feet up on the desk, and gazed out the window onto the town square below. It was only mid-morning, but already a sweltering August day with both the temperature and humidity hovering above ninety. An afternoon shower seemed inevitable. But it wasn't the weather that had him perspiring. Worries filled his thoughts. Did he use Jennings in an inappropriate way? What if Jo says no? What if she says yes?

"Knock. Knock."

"Oh, hi Beverly. What's up?" Ben said in response to the words Beverly used occasionally to interrupt his musing when he didn't notice her standing in his office doorway.

"Me intruding into your personal life."

"How so?"

"Telling you your lovely wife needs a night out. Tonight's as good a night as any."

"But we have Danielle."

"And in me you have a grandmother of six. I've spoken with Marla. I'll be at your house at five-thirty. You have reservations at Main Fare at six."

Ben waited until they'd enjoyed their first glass of chardonnay and the appetizers had been served before beginning the journals update Marla eagerly anticipated.

"So even though Jo invited you and Danielle, we *are* going there under false pretenses. I hope we can create an appropriate segue from business with me to a book discussion with you."

"Not having met her, I think *hope* is an appropriate word choice. But I have complete confidence in your persuasive abilities. And your Southern charm."

"Sorry, my dear. I'm just the door-opener in this little endeavor. You're the closer."

"I take back what I just said."

"About what?"

"Your charm. Seriously, at least we'll have our answer in two days' time, as we Australians say."

"Marla, here's a thought. Telling her she named her company after your birthplace might be a nice way to begin your conversation."

"Great idea. And I promise you it will be a fair dinkum meeting."

"A fair what?

"It's Australian. Look it up."

After they arrived home, and Beverly had departed, Marla remembered that cryptic remark Ben made the night before. "Ben, you told me there were two disappointments when you met with Jennings yesterday. One was the book idea. What was the other?"

"That Jennings is going to follow my father's example and retire early next year."

"Why's that a disappointment? Weren't you anticipating his retirement with all the planning you've been doing?"

"But not this soon. And since I've been planning to leave the company when he did, I was hoping for at least another year to transition."

"Transition to what? To another job?"

"In a manner of speaking." After hesitating, he continued, "I've been giving thought to running for Congress."

"As in Washington, D.C.?"

"Yes," Ben answered hesitantly. "I haven't mentioned it before since the mid-term election isn't for another couple of years. I thought we had plenty of time to discuss it, and we still do. Sorry to spring all this on you now. Certainly not what I'd planned."

Before Marla could respond, their daughter announced her need for immediate attention. Marla was struck by how this was becoming a recurring factor in her life – her daughter's needs suddenly interrupting serious conversations with her husband. But she was thankful for this one, since it gave her time to collect her thoughts.

Years ago, Ben had been elected to the Kentucky House of Representatives, and was widely regarded, at the time, as a rising political player. Then he suddenly resigned midway during his second term in office following Lauren's stroke. But *this* was different, much different, Marla thought as she sat rocking Danielle.

If Ben were to be elected, something Marla thought was entirely possible, she knew it would be the end of her dream to return to the university. How could she resume her university career while raising a small child with a husband spending much of his time away from home? It was the sacrifice so many women choose to make, or have to make – allowing their aspirations to become secondary to their commitments to husbands and children. But not one Marla had seriously contemplated for herself.

At that moment, Marla resolved that crossing the line between supporting her husband and sacrificing her dreams would be negotiable in her marriage – not a given. Her resolution lasted only a few days.

9

Thursday morning, Ben and Marla waited as the solid two-piece gate opened slowly, then drove along a winding driveway lined with mature oak trees, Jo's Bardstown house not yet visible. Ben commented on the similarity to the thirteen-acre estate of Elvis Presley in Memphis they'd visited a year ago, except the Graceland mansion could be seen from the road.

They drove slowly up the hill, and when they crested, came upon a circular driveway. Given the sense of arrival they'd just experienced, they were anticipating a mansion. What appeared before them was a large, well-maintained late 1800s residence, but certainly not a mansion.

Ben parked in front of the house, and as they were getting out of the car, a man stepped out onto the covered porch. At least six-foot-two, dressed in an expensive black suit with a black collarless shirt, he was the picture-perfect, physical embodiment of what the author in Ben and Marla would have described as either a former professional athlete or a bodyguard. With either choice, they would have been correct.

"Good morning, and welcome. My name is Richard. I'm Jo's assistant. May I help you with anything?"

Ben later told Marla he thought Richard's voice was as smooth and articulate as any network newscaster he'd ever heard. Marla had noticed everything *but* his voice.

The two-story house was of the same beautiful white Bedford stone as the entrance, and looked as if it had just been pressure-washed. Green shutters framed each of the large windows, and two chimneys gave the appearance of bookends framing a copper roof gleaming in the morning sunlight. A large weather vane featuring a galloping horse sat atop the chimney on the right.

"Jo asked me to extend her apologies, and tell you an unexpected call is running long. It should only be a few more minutes. Please make yourselves comfortable," Richard said, gesturing toward an oversized brown leather sofa.

They were in the parlor, a large tray laden with orange juice, water and an assortment of small scones already on the coffee table. As Richard leaned forward and began pouring coffee, his suit coat opened slightly and both Marla and Ben glimpsed a large handgun in a shoulder holster.

"I am so sorry, and so embarrassed, to have kept you waiting," Jo said, as she hurriedly entered the room, "and in my home of all places. Please accept my apology."

Rising, Ben extended his hand to greet her, and said, "No apology necessary. Richard has taken great care of us."

"That's very kind of you, Ben, but I'm embarrassed nonetheless. And you, of course, are Marla. It's a great pleasure to meet you. Thank you for coming this morning."

Cradling the baby in her left arm, Marla reached up with her right hand as Jo extended hers in greeting. Jo knelt down in front of Marla, adding, "And for bringing Danielle. It was a selfish request for me to make, but a rare treat for me to have a baby in my house."

As Jo sat in a chair opposite the sofa, she smoothed out a wrinkle in her skirt. Jo's tan two-piece St. Johns Knits suit and silk scarf complemented her caramel-colored complexion that was framed by perfectly coiffed, shoulder-length hair. Marla thought to herself that this beautiful woman had exquisite, and expensive, taste. Everything about their surroundings and their hostess gave the impression of understated wealth. And class.

"Before we get to business, I know you have to be curious about Richard. But let me first ask. Marla, do you know what's going to happen with my company? And the donation to the foundation?" Uncertain how to respond, Marla looked at Ben before answering. Jo couldn't help noticing. "Oh, it's okay if Ben tells you everything. I would expect him to. I just don't want to bore you with things you already know."

"Yes, Ben told me. I think it's wonderfully generous of you. For your employees, and for all the children who'll be helped."

"And you know about my relationship with Ben's father and Jennings Eldridge?"

"I don't know any details," Marla replied, "but I do know they've been an important part of your life. And you in theirs."

"Well, I asked because it helps explain Richard. And his colleagues."

"How so?" Ben asked.

"He's one of five security professionals I employ at the insistence of both your father and Jennings. I'm never without one of them. In my home. At the office. When I travel. It's been this way for many years."

"Why?" Ben asked.

"Being a woman, and more specifically, a woman of, shall we say, means, they were worried about kidnapping in addition to the unpleasant things that can happen to *any* woman. But since I'm the sole owner of my company, responsible for the livelihoods of over a thousand employees and their families, the concern extends well beyond just me."

"I can see the need," Marla said, "and it's unfortunate. But don't you find it terribly intrusive? I think I would."

"At first, I fought the idea. But it was Ben's father who was especially insistent. Even after all these years, I'm still embarrassed out in public, how people regard me when they see me being handled like a celebrity. But in accepting the need, I learned to live with it. I refer to them as my guardian angels."

"Jo," Marla said, "other than his physical appearance, I would have never guessed Richard to be a bodyguard. He's so well-mannered and articulate. Or maybe he's just the first bodyguard I've ever had offer to carry diapers and serve me coffee."

"And he's easy on the eyes, isn't he?" Jo asked.

"Yes, he is!"

"Ladies, I'm still here," Ben interjected.

"Yes you *are*, Ben," Jo said, "and with your lovely wife present, may I say I find you easy on the eyes, as well?"

"Yes, you may," Ben answered, returning her smile.

"Seriously," Jo said, "it's important for you to know all five are church-going family men employed by a company in which Jennings is a substantial investor."

Marla instantly understood why Jo had provided that additional information, but it appeared lost on Ben as he was opening his brief-case and withdrawing some papers. Marla then remembered Jo's insistence that Danielle accompany them, and how special she said her presence was after they arrived.

"Jo, would you like to hold Danielle?"

For a moment, Marla thought Jo was going to cry.

"May I?" Jo finally said as she stood up.

"Of course. It might be easiest if you sit in the rocking chair. It'll give your arm support, and hopefully she'll stay asleep."

The baby, wrapped in a pink blanket, was slowly handed to the waiting arms of a woman with the most radiant smile Marla thought she'd ever seen.

Jo settled in with Danielle and turned her attention to Ben, answering his prepared questions and the additional ones her answers prompted. Almost an hour later, he told her he had what he came for.

"Ben," Jo said, as he was closing his briefcase, "when you called yesterday, you said there was something else. Something you were doing with Jennings you wanted to discuss."

After briefly explaining how he learned about and read Jennings' journals, Ben explained his journals-to-book idea.

"That sounds interesting," Jo said, "but I'm surprised to hear Jennings is comfortable making his journals public."

"Jennings turned me down," Ben said, hesitantly. "At least for now. He wants us to remain focused on business matters, especially yours, and he's not comfortable with any publicity that would call attention to him."

"I'm not surprised. But is this what you wanted to discuss with me?"

"No," Ben answered. "In talking with Jennings, I guessed correctly that his mentoring influence meant you also keep similar journals."

"Well, that's true," Jo said. A few seconds passed before she continued. "Am I to assume you want to ask me to agree to something Jennings didn't?"

Ben didn't pick up on Jo's change in demeanor and tone of voice, but Marla did.

"Yes," he answered. "He gave me permission to tell you he told me, and he knows we're going to suggest the same book idea to you."

"We? As in you and Jennings?"

"No. That's where I come in," Marla said, hoping to keep Jo from getting upset with Ben by diverting her focus. And to take ownership of *her* idea, regardless of the outcome. "I'm offering my assistance to you in much the same way as Ben would have assisted Jennings."

"I'm sorry," Jo said, with a look of obvious puzzlement, "and I really don't mean this in an unkind way. But it would be helpful to understand your qualifications to write a book. For either Jennings or me."

Marla and Ben looked at each other and realized they'd both jumped headlong into a discussion without any foundation. In his only meeting with Jo, Ben hadn't shared anything about his writing success. And in talking about Marla, he'd only said she was a professor on maternity leave. Nothing about her books, or her work as a professional writing coach and editor that helped him achieve best-seller status.

After apologizing profusely, Marla tried to quickly cover their literary landscape. But the more she tried, the more tongue-tied and embarrassed she became. Partly because of how stupidly presumptuous they'd been. But also because she was intimidated by this poised, beautiful woman.

"Marla, please don't apologize," Jo said. "I can't tell you how many times I've gotten ahead of myself. Happens to all of us, so not to worry. I just want to understand what you're proposing."

Not for one minute did Marla believe this woman ever made such a clumsy faux pas, but she greatly appreciated the class and kindness Jo demonstrated in trying to put her at ease. Ben's expression was one that urged Marla to let him take over, but since she didn't sense he'd yet grasped the consequences of their ready-fire-aim approach, she kept going.

"The idea isn't fully developed, but essentially it involves lifting material from your journals into a book to inspire others in their pursuit of success. You could be the author, with my help, or I could write a book about you."

"If I understand correctly, either way the publicity Jennings wants to avoid would come my way."

"Yes," Ben answered.

"Jo," Marla added quickly, "it's the success you've achieved that gives the book credibility. Without you, we don't see the idea being viable."

"Marla, from what you've told me, I believe I'd be in good hands with you. But this isn't something I'd ever given any thought to. I hope you'll understand I need some time before giving you an answer."

"Certainly," Marla replied, grateful the conversation was ending. "Are you still okay holding Danielle? I don't want her to be a burden."

"How could this precious child possibly be a burden? Well, maybe when she's a teenager, but that's for another time, isn't it? Seriously, I can't describe how wonderful this feels. Thank you."

They all sat quietly. Although Ben and Marla had nothing left to discuss, Jo didn't seem in any hurry for them to leave.

"There is one more thing. Ben, after you shared your story the other day, I sent you to your father and Jennings to ask about mine. You may have thought it strange, or unfair, but did you?"

"I did."

"What did they tell you?"

"Knowing both of them as you do, they didn't go into a lot of detail. I know a little bit about your childhood, and that you went to work with Jennings' company before starting your own. By doing the financial analysis on your company, I know how successful you've become. Oh, and it was your advocacy for at-risk children that led them to share your decision about our foundation."

After a few moments of awkward silence, with her eyes looking down at Danielle, Jo asked, "Anything else?"

"No, not that I recall. But it's obvious they think the world of you."

"And I of them," she answered, now looking at her guests.

Marla immediately sensed that Jo asking if there was "anything else" while not maintaining eye contact meant there *was*. Something important. She didn't sense Ben picked up on it, so maybe there was something to the gender intuition thing after all. But both of them were surprised when Jo returned to the book discussion.

"I hope you understand I need to devote all of my time, for now, to the company transition. As Ben knows, it's all moving as quickly as possible, and we're hoping it'll be completed by the end of the year. Time is not on our side. I'll then step aside, with no further involvement."

She was obviously going somewhere with this, so neither Ben nor Marla spoke.

"While my answer today about the book is a maybe, and not the yes you came seeking, I want you to know I'll give it serious consideration. It may be just the thing to fill a big void in my life after the first of the year."

"I know we surprised you this morning, so we completely understand," Ben answered.

"Ben, I know you were enthusiastic about Jennings' journals, but mine may prove to be a real disappointment. So here's a thought. Unlike his, which are still handwritten, mine have all been converted to Word documents. So, Marla, I can email them to you tomorrow. Once you've read them, or even a small portion, you may decide the book idea isn't viable, and you won't offend me."

"I don't think for one minute that's the conclusion I'll reach," Marla said, "but I certainly have the time to read them. I can then be much better prepared to help you when you're ready to begin. Assuming, of course, you decide to begin. Which I hope you do."

"If we decide to do this, you must understand I'll be totally dependent upon you. Primarily, of course, because I'm not a writer, you are. And other reasons."

Marla was pleased with the direction the conversation had turned, and even sensed an unexpected urgency in what Jo had just shared. Danielle began to stir, and as Jo moved her arm slightly from its resting place on the rocking chair's arm, the Taylor's precious daughter threw up, somehow missing the blanket entirely and hitting Jo's chest.

Before Ben and Marla could utter apologies, Jo, smiling and looking down at Danielle, said, "Well, you must feel better now, little one."

Ben handed Marla the diaper bag, and when she returned a few minutes later, Jo and Ben were standing in the foyer, a signal the meeting had concluded. The impression their daughter had made on Jo was still visible, and Marla started to say something, but Jo anticipated and spoke first.

"As I told Ben, one of the advantages of owning a cleaning products company is knowing what to do when these situations arise. Although my previous experiences have all been the result of an inability to hold my liquor."

Did Marla think Jo Gilpin had ever gotten drunk and thrown up on herself? Not in a million years. Did she think she was a model of perfection in making others feel at ease in awkward situations? Absolutely.

Standing on the front porch, Jo thanked them again for coming, hugging first Marla and then Ben, turning slightly so as to not transfer Danielle's breakfast to them. Yes was the answer both Ben and Marla gave at the same time when Jo asked if she could kiss Danielle on the forehead.

Ben held the door open for Danielle and Marla, then walked around the front of the car to the driver's side, and stood facing the porch. "Jo, thank you again for this morning. I'll call when I need more time with you. Will that be alright?"

"Of course, Ben. As long as you continue to meet my two conditions."

Ben responded by pointing to the two occupants in the car.

"Yes. Drive carefully."

Jo remained on the porch to wave as Ben and Marla began the slow drive toward the entrance. Neither of them spoke during the few minutes it took to reach the on-ramp to the Bluegrass Parkway for the journey home. In the quiet, Marla was overtaken with a feeling that her life would never be the same

10

"Jo Gilpin's on the phone," Beverly said, standing in the doorway to Jennings' office. "She called for Ben to get Marla's email address. Did you want to tell her?"

"Yes," he answered softly, standing and straightening his suit coat. This was not a conversation he was going to have sitting down. He picked up the phone on the first ring when it was transferred.

"Jennings, I didn't mean for Beverly to interrupt you, but it's always a joy to talk with you."

"Jo," he said, his voice gaining strength, "I'm afraid things aren't very joyous around here right now. Ben and Marla's baby daughter is in the hospital, and things aren't looking good."

"Oh, my God!" Jo exclaimed. "What happened?"

"I don't know that much. Marla became concerned about Danielle after they got home from Bardstown yesterday."

"Concerned about what?" Jo interrupted. She was calling from her office and, like Jennings, was now standing.

"I only talked with Ben for a few minutes early this morning. He said the baby wasn't active, and her coloring didn't look good. They did what many first-time parents would and took her to the emergency room. Good thing they did – she's in intensive care."

"Intensive care!" Jo exclaimed. "Does that mean they know what's wrong?"

"No. Ben told me they said it could be any of a number of things, so they're taking her by ambulance to Riley Children's Hospital in Indianapolis."

"Jennings, I want to help. That's a four-hour trip in the best of circumstances, and the interstate is torn up and only one lane several places south of Louisville." As she began pacing back and forth, a solution came to her. "Give me ten minutes," she said forcefully, "and I'll call you back."

Ninety minutes later, Ben was standing on the tarmac at the Bowling Green airport, watching the lights of a plane approaching from the southwest. Marla was in the back of the ambulance with Danielle. After landing, in less than twenty minutes the large private jet was once again airborne, headed north to Indianapolis. On board were the three Taylors, as well as a pediatric nurse and a paramedic.

When they arrived at the Indianapolis International Airport, a young woman with a starched white coat indicating she was a doctor from Riley supervised Danielle's transfer from the airplane to a fully-equipped ambulance. The elapsed time from leaving the Bowling Green hospital to Danielle undergoing an initial examination at a world-renowned children's hospital had been less than two hours.

"Jennings, Jo Gilpin is calling for you again."

"Thank you, Beverly. Put her through."

Jennings listened as Jo gave him the update, ending with her confirmation Danielle and her parents had arrived at the Indianapolis hospital.

"Jo, you're a miracle worker. How did you make all that happen?"

"Not difficult, really. My first thought was our company plane, but it was a couple of hours away and heading in the wrong direction. So I called a friend in Nashville who provides private jet service for country music entertainers, and commandeered one of his planes."

"Well, it was a wonderful gesture. Allow me to cut in line ahead of Marla and Ben in thanking you."

"Jennings," Jo said, with an unmistakable tone of seriousness in her voice, "I've just met Ben and Marla. And Danielle. I'm worried this may be my fault."

"Your fault. What do you mean?"

"I practically insisted they bring Danielle to the meeting with me yesterday. Maybe the trip was too much for her."

"Oh, Jo, I think the doctors will confirm that's not even the remotest possibility."

"Still, I'd like to do more to help. Can you think of anything?"

"Here's a thought," Jennings answered. "The Judge is leaving soon to join them. He's in Frankfort. Why don't you call him and offer him a ride. Your security man can drive, and I'm certain you can be a comfort to The Judge."

"I'll call him right now. And if we do go together, I'll let you know what's happening as soon as we know."

It was early afternoon when The Judge and Jo arrived at Riley Hospital. Although none of Jennings' businesses extended north of the Mason-Dixon Line, his reputation and connections did. He rarely exerted his influence, but on this occasion the hospital's CEO was alerted by Jennings to the impending arrival of two of Kentucky's most prominent citizens. The Judge and Jo were met by a waiting senior member of the hospital administration, and within minutes were sitting next to Marla and Ben in a seventh-floor waiting room.

"The doctors say it's too early for them to know anything for certain," Ben said, "but we had time to pack clothes, so we're here for the duration."

"Have the two of you eaten anything today?" Jo asked.

When both Ben and Marla shook their heads, Jo said, "Why don't the three of you go down to the cafeteria. I'll wait here. Just tell the nurse at the desk they can let me know if there's a development, and I'll come get you."

They returned about forty-five minutes later, with Ben stopping at the reception desk to sign some additional forms as The Judge escorted Marla down the hall toward the waiting room. As he turned away from the desk, Ben couldn't help overhearing a hushed conversation between two nurses.

"Who is she?" the first one asked.

"Don't know, but she sure is beautiful," the second nurse answered. "And probably famous."

"Famous? How do you know?"

"Well, she *looks* like a celebrity, and a friend in security told me that handsome black man – the one who came in with her and the older white man – is a bodyguard."

"How do they know he's a bodyguard?"

"He told them. Had to – he's carrying a gun in a hospital."

The intensive care night shift transitioned in shortly before eleven, and the lead physician walked into the waiting room. The only occupants were Marla, Ben, The Judge and Jo. Another guardian angel had driven in from Versailles to relieve his colleague, and positioned himself in a chair down the hallway.

The doctor said they wouldn't have new test results until sometime the following morning, and advised them to get some sleep. Ben and Marla had reservations at the Hyatt Hotel a few minutes' walking distance from the hospital. The Judge and Jo accompanied them as they checked-in, then said their good-byes and walked back to the hospital parking garage. They were followed a discrete few steps behind by the security man who would drive them back to Frankfort first, ending up at Jo's Bardstown home.

Exhausted but not sleepy, Marla wanted to talk about anything that would give her mind a rest from worrying about Danielle. They hadn't finished their conversation about Ben's possible political aspirations, but that would have to wait for another time. Then she remembered a recurring thought, something she'd sensed, and decided to ask.

"Ben, is there something more to Jo's friendship with your father than hers with Jennings?"

Marla was reclining against the headrest on one of the two queen-sized beds in their spacious hotel room. Ben was sitting in one of the casual chairs, looking out the window when he turned to answer.

"I'm not certain what you mean."

"I'm not certain I know either. I just sensed something watching them together today."

"Are you suggesting romantic?"

"Well, yes, I guess I am. And I don't mean to upset you."

"It's not upsetting. Far from it. I've often wondered myself. But if they do have those feelings for each other, I doubt they've acted on them. I don't think *that's* something they could hide, nor do I think they would try to."

"If it's true, how do you feel about it?" Marla asked.

"You mean, would it bother me if my father was in love with a black woman my age?"

Marla's expression conveyed that Ben guessed correctly. Her nod confirmed it.

"The simple, and completely honest, answer is no. Any happiness my father can find in the years he has remaining, he should have. And their ages should have nothing to do with it."

"And the other?"

"Marla, my father raised me to believe the world should be color-blind when it comes to all God's children. And his legal career is living testimony to that belief. My best friend in Chicago, and now in Bowling Green since he moved there to coach track at Western, is African American."

"Charles Upshaw," Marla said knowingly, referring to their frequent houseguest and her husband's Pilates instructor.

"Now, I'm not going to lie to you and say I don't see the racial difference with Charles or Jo when I'm with them, but it doesn't matter. To either my father, or me."

"If you've had the same sense as me about your father and Jo, why have you never said anything to him?"

"For fear of being wrong, and embarrassing him."

"I understand," Marla said, though she didn't. It was something she felt fairly certain most daughters would ask their mother, or a woman would ask another woman. If they were close friends, that is.

While Ben was taking a shower, Marla felt she was losing any semblance of control over her life. Her daughter's health was suddenly precarious, and her husband's future plans could create storm clouds over hers.

Her thoughts turned to Jo Gilpin, and she wondered if this woman who had just entered her life in such a significant way had ever *not* been in total control of the events in her life. She remembered Ben's retelling of the lunch conversation in which his father and Jennings had shared, at Jo's encouragement, details about her life. Marla's response to Ben at the time was, "Lots of layers, and likely many more." Little did Marla, or any of them, know.

11

August 23, 1994

"Say that again."

"Jo, Winston Collins is married."

"And you know this how?" Jo said, surprise and anger mixed together in her voice.

A few minutes earlier, Charlie Flener had stopped the car in front of her house after driving her home from the office late one summer afternoon. Charlie said he had something important to tell her, and asked if he could come inside for a few minutes.

Jo admired and respected all the men in her security detail, but Charlie was a special guardian angel. He was older, in his late 50s, and a former police chaplain. He was the first she'd hired, and over time had become someone in whom she confided things she wouldn't, or couldn't, share with others.

In Charlie, she had someone to talk to when feeling angry, negative, bitter or resentful. In other words, when she was being human. Charlie's wife Ruth was a professionally trained counselor with a doctorate degree, and sometimes Jo felt her issues rose to needing that kind of confidential help. Charlie and Ruth had seen a person Jo had kept hidden from everyone else, including Jennings and The Judge.

Charlie's shift was officially over, and his colleague David had opened the front door when they arrived. As they entered the house,

Charlie said, "David, Jo and I need a few minutes to finish a conversation. We'll be in the parlor."

They sat facing each other on the sofa, and it seemed like an eternity before Charlie spoke.

"Ruth and I were guests at a charity function last night in Cincinnati. Winston and his wife were among the dinner guests in the audience recognized by one of the speakers."

Jo had met Winston at a Christmas party in Lexington seven months earlier. He was handsome, sophisticated, and charming, and she felt an immediate attraction. They exchanged business cards, and he called the next day. That call was followed by a dinner date a few evenings later, and their romance began.

"How do you know she was his wife? Could've been someone else. A colleague, maybe." Jo's mind wasn't yet willing to accept what she'd just heard.

Winston lived in Cincinnati and, like Jo, had a very full professional calendar. They both traveled extensively, and Jo appreciated his insistence on meeting her in Versailles or Bardstown when their schedules permitted. And on occasions when their travel schedules aligned, they would meet in other cities. Jo had always kept her personal and professional lives separate, and her growing relationship with Winston seemed like a perfect fit.

"They were introduced as Mr. and Mrs. Winston Collins and asked to stand."

"And you're sure it was him?" She was grasping at faint hope that was rapidly slipping away. His answer was a nod. With her recognition of Winston's betrayal came anger, and Charlie took the brunt of it.

"Why are you telling me this now?" she asked, her voice cracking and her lip quivering. "You couldn't wait even an entire day before telling me that I've been made a complete fool of by a man I thought I might marry?"

"Because he knows I saw him. I was sitting at a nearby table, and Winston looked right at me as his wife was settling back into her chair."

"Did you talk to him?"

"No. It wouldn't have been our place. Ruth's or mine."

"Did he make any attempt to speak with you?"

"Jo, he never looked my way again, and he couldn't get out of that room fast enough when the event was over."

Jo had often marveled at Winston's casual acceptance of her security team. One of them was always discretely with them when they dined out or went to functions. Even to the occasional movie. And, of course, when she travelled. They were at her home in Bardstown when Winston was with her for a "sleepover."

Jennings and The Judge were aware of her relationship with Winston because she'd shared her happiness with them. The Judge suggested she consider a professional background check, something she'd filed away for future consideration.

"Damn it. Damn it to hell!" Jo shouted.

Hearing her, David came running into the room. She assured him everything was okay, just venting about a business deal that wasn't working out. After David withdrew, she finally lost her composure and collapsed sobbing into Charlie's comforting arms.

With the tears came an outpouring of bitterness she couldn't control. Charlie patiently listened as she angrily rehashed things he already knew. That she'd never had a father, or siblings. That her success meant she'd lost the freedom to be just like any other woman, at least in finding someone to love, to be married to, to hold her at night.

"I thought I'd finally found someone not interested in me for my money, someone willing to accept all that goes with me being me.

Including you, Charlie, and the others. With your guns. And everything. That's what I thought I had in Winston. And I desperately want at least one child, to love as my mother loved me."

"I know you're hurting," Charlie said, "and I want to help. But I'm out of my depth. Do you want to talk with Ruth?"

"No! Right now, I'm embarrassed enough with just you knowing. Charlie, I confess I've never in my life been this angry. I don't like how it feels, or what I'm thinking now."

"What are you thinking?"

"Can I borrow your gun? Not for very long. Only until I find that son of a bitch. You know, I don't even have his home address. All I have is his business card. How fuck'n trusting is that?"

Sitting back up, and noticing Charlie's questioning expression, Jo asked, "What are you looking at?"

"I'm looking at a woman I'd thought I'd do anything for. But loaning her my gun isn't gonna happen."

"Well, we both know I wasn't being serious. Not completely, anyway. But why are you still looking at me like that?"

"Because you are the most intelligent, most sophisticated, most articulate woman I've ever known. Ruth agrees."

"And?" she asked, impatiently.

"Well, I never doubted you knew the F word. I just didn't think the first time I ever heard you say it, it would be the shortened version."

"Are you fuck'n, excuse me, *fuck-ing* kidding me? That's what you're thinking at *this* moment? When you've just turned my world upside down?"

"I see your point. If I were you, I wouldn't have chosen 'flippin' or 'friggin' either."

"Do you think that makes either of us less of a Christian?" Jo asked, with genuine concern in her voice.

"Not in the least. Jo, an occasional profanity couldn't possibly put the slightest dent in who you are, the person we all know you to be. It just means you're human, like the rest of us."

"You're not offended? Not disappointed in me?"

"Of course not. Would it make you feel any better if I said the word right now? It would make us even, at least in this conversation, and we could move on."

Charlie and Jo looked each other for a few seconds, then they began laughing.

"No, Charlie, you save the word for when *you* need it."

Charlie could tell from Jo's expression that she was now thinking intently about something, so he asked, "What's going on behind those beautiful eyes now?"

"I was just wondering what I should do about Winston." She was quiet for a few moments, then asked, "Charlie, do by any chance have a big knife, hopefully one not too sharp? Maybe with some rust on it."

"Let's let that one pass, and keep thinking," Charlie answered.

"You got any better ideas?" she asked.

"I do."

After that event in Cincinnati, Winston never called. Whenever Jo thought of him, negative words replaced the previously positive ones, with *coward* foremost among them.

Winston Collins was a professional political operative working on a national level. His work, and promoting his books. resulted in a robust schedule of compensated speaking engagements around the country. Without sharing with Jennings or The Judge, Jo acted on Charlie's suggestion and authorized the security firm to begin following Winston. It didn't take but a few months for her to learn she wasn't the only foolish woman in his universe. In one of the surveillance reports she read, one of the investigators referred to him as a "real whore dog." Charlie tried to suppress a smile when telling her this was an official term in the world of private eyes.

It took more digging, and more time, for them to determine Winston had leveraged, without her knowledge, his personal relationship with Jo to open fundraising doors she never would have approved. When the time was right, she began making discrete phone calls to close those doors. She learned later, and indirectly, that she had set off the pleasantly surprising, but unintended, consequence of creating a domino effect. Winston became a pariah in his chosen field of endeavor – the one that had allowed him to travel around the country, using his lavish expense account to prey on countless unsuspecting women, including some who were married.

The investigators were fairly certain Winston's wife was as clueless as Jo had been. The Collins didn't have children, and Jo felt obligated to do something. Completely untraceable to her, a copy of the entire file, in all its detail, including photos, was delivered by courier to the office of Winston's wife. Since she was a successful litigation attorney, Jo figured she could take care of herself legally, if she chose to do something. And maybe, Jo allowed herself to think, Mrs. Collins would consider the rusty knife option.

12

The early Saturday morning sun streamed through the window as Marla and Ben dressed to return to the hospital. They both felt reasonably refreshed after several hours of exhaustion-induced sleep, but their apprehension about what lay ahead weighed as heavily as it must have on other parents of tiny patients at Riley who had also spent one or more nights in the same hotel room.

When Marla and Ben arrived at the reception desk on the floor where their daughter had spent the night, a young nurse escorted them to a small conference room and told them a doctor would be with them momentarily.

"Momentarily" in hospital parlance could be anything, but mercifully it was only about ten minutes before two physicians, a man and a woman, entered the room. Marla recognized the woman as the doctor who had met their plane when it arrived in Indianapolis the day before.

"What can you tell us?" Ben asked the moment the doctors entered the room, his abrupt words revealing the apprehension that had built up in both he and Marla overnight.

The male doctor was obviously older and carried himself with more of an air of authority than his colleague, but it was the woman doctor who spoke. She told them Danielle was improving rapidly, and that they anticipated a full recovery without consequences.

"That's wonderful!" Marla exclaimed.

"Recovery from what?" Ben asked, impatiently.

"We're waiting for some test results tomorrow, but we're almost certain your daughter has RSV – respiratory syncytial virus. Here, I've written the name down for you," she said, handing Marla a small note paper used for writing prescriptions.

"It's a respiratory infection afflicting infants," the young physician continued, "and rarely results in hospitalization. Your daughter fell into the two percent requiring the kind of care she's receiving. You were wise to take her to the Bowling Green hospital as soon as you did."

"Your decision to fly her here instead of driving may have been a life-saving one," the other physician said, speaking for the first time.

"Life saving?" Ben asked. "Danielle was *that* sick? What do you mean?"

Realizing that her colleague had left any semblance of a comforting bedside manner at home that morning, the woman doctor spoke before he could.

"Mr. and Mrs. Taylor, it was possible the RSV could have resulted in a very serious case of pneumonia, and that's not something every infant can survive. We have no way of knowing, of course. We're just glad you brought her to us as quickly as you did."

Several more minutes of questions and answers concluded with the physicians saying that if the tests results confirmed their diagnosis, then they wanted to keep Danielle for a few more days of observation. Just to be sure.

Left alone in the room, Marla and Ben held hands, and cried. Marla whispered a prayer that what the doctors *thought* today would turn out to be reality tomorrow. As she opened her eyes, she felt a familiar sense of calm come over her, briefly but powerfully. From previous experiences in the past, she knew to pay attention to it.

Drying her tears, Marla said, "Ben, if what they said about the urgency to get Danielle here was true, then that life-saving decision was not ours. Or at least it wouldn't have been ours if Jo hadn't suggested it, and made it happen."

"I know," Ben answered, "and I'm ashamed to admit I didn't thank her when she was here."

"Me neither," Marla said, "but hopefully she understood, given the circumstances. I'm going to call her now to make certain. I don't know how we can ever repay her."

While Marla was on her cell phone with Jo, Ben used his to call both his father and Jennings with the update. All three offered to come to Indianapolis, but were told to spend the weekend at home and see what Monday brought.

After several hospital cafeteria meals, Marla and Ben treated themselves to a Sunday evening dinner at the upscale restaurant in the Hyatt. Their appetites had become a casualty of the worry about their daughter, and they mostly picked at their food. But the different atmosphere, especially the quiet, was a change they both appreciated. And both wanted a break from focusing entirely on the medical emergency.

"Ben, I was just wondering. Since Jo's not from Versailles, do you know why she located her company there?"

"I do, but only because I asked Jennings. Versailles is reasonably close to almost half the country's population, which makes it easier to distribute the products she manufactures. And Lexington being nearby is a plus in recruiting executives not familiar with the state."

"I didn't think to ask her when we talked earlier. Was that her plane we flew on?"

"No," Ben answered. "Jennings told me she first tried to get her own plane, but it was out west somewhere." He then told her how Jo had secured their transportation.

"Isn't having her own plane somewhat out of character for Jo?" Marla asked.

"One would think. Usually they're an expensive luxury feeding executive egos. But for Jo, it became a necessity."

"Why?"

"Jennings told me that as her company grew, she faced an increasing need for her and her executives to travel to places difficult to reach with scheduled airlines. The plane eliminates a lot of wasted travel time. It scoops her executives up from various locations around the country and has them back on Friday afternoon so they can spend weekends with their families. It gets serviced at the Blue Grass Airport near her headquarters to be ready again on Monday morning."

"Must be a big plane."

"Jo's a pragmatist. It's big enough to accommodate their needs, but not so big it can't land at any of the airports they need to reach. It's even been to Bowling Green when she's on her way to or from a more distant location. Otherwise, she'd drive down."

"Why does Jo have to travel? Can't she just depend on others?"

"Jo has always has been the company's leader in business development. Jennings says she's the best he's ever seen, male or female, in any industry."

Their waiter cleared away their partially eaten meals, and received an affirmative answer when he asked if they'd like to see the desert menu. After he departed, Marla asked, "Ben, I'll understand if you can't answer, but is Jo's company in trouble?"

"The short answer is no. What made you ask?"

"Several things she said. Or didn't say."

"Like what?"

"Remember when she asked if your father and Jennings had told you anything else?" Ben nodded. "Well, I'm certain she asked the question because there *is* something else."

"If there is, it could be anything," Ben answered.

"And she said she'd have nothing to do with her company after the transition. She specifically said not as an advisor or a board member."

"I heard that, too. And as I think about it now, it would be unusual to just completely walk away from her creation. Her life's work. That *is* strange."

"Ben, I think it's more than just strange. I've never owned a business, but I don't see how she can emotionally disconnect that easily, and that quickly."

"I'm with you. Anything else?"

Before she could answer, the waiter returned with the desert menus and waited for them to make their selection. They decided to share a piece of chocolate cake the menu described as decadent, accompanied by decaf cappuccino for each of them.

"She said 'time is not on our side,'" Marla continued after the waiter departed.

"*That* I don't remember hearing. Do you remember the context?"

"It was when she was talking about the timeframe to complete the company transition."

"It may be that she's tired of all the details, of meetings like the one with me, and just wants it to be over."

"Or it could be she has serious health issues."

"But Marla, she looks perfectly healthy."

"I know. Well, all I know is she's a fascinating woman, and I hope I'll get to know her better."

Another nagging thought had entered Marla's mind. Jo went from being surprised and initially lukewarm about the book idea, to offering to send her journals the next day.

"Ben, when Jo talked about the book maybe happening, she said she would be totally dependent upon me."

"She said it herself. *You're* the writer."

"But then she said 'and other reasons.' Remember?"

"I do. So what do you think all this means?" Ben asked.

"No idea. Maybe it's nothing. But if there *is* something, or more than one something, I'll never know unless we're working together on the book."

"And if you are, you think she'll tell you?"

"Yes. Not at first. Over time."

"You seem awfully certain. You barely know her."

"But, my darling, I know *me*."

Monday morning, the doctors informed them the tests confirmed their RSV diagnosis, and that it would be best if Danielle remained at Riley until Friday. Ben called his father with the update, then Jennings, and ultimately Jo.

"Ben," Jo said, "do you have any idea what time you would be leaving on Friday?"

"Unless her condition takes a turn for the worse, the doctor told us we can leave by mid-day."

"I hope and pray it does happen," Jo said, "and this helps me."

"I don't know what you mean."

"You will. And soon. I'll call you later this morning."

Ben picked up his cell phone when it began vibrating at almost exactly eleven, and saw Jo's name on the caller ID. Jo said she'd arranged a return flight home for them and wanted to give him the details.

"Jo, that's a kind and generous offer, but an unnecessary one. And costly. We can rent a car and drive home. But thank you."

"Ben, I doubt the doctors will let you do that, and an ambulance ride down I-65 in Kentucky with all the construction would not be pleasant. I want to do this for all of you, especially Danielle, so please let me tell you what I've arranged before you say no."

Jo had called her friend in Nashville, and he'd confirmed there was space on a private charter bringing another entertainer back to Nashville from Boston Friday afternoon. A brief stop in Indianapolis wouldn't be a problem. Then she told Ben the name of the entertainer.

"Jo, I don't know what to say. She's Marla's favorite singer. No one is even close. If this does happen, can we keep it a secret until we get on the plane? Marla will be thrilled, and after all she's been through this week, she needs the boost."

At almost exactly noon on Friday, a chauffeured Town Car with the Taylors in the backseat glided through traffic on the I-465 beltway encircling Indianapolis. As the car approached the exit that would take them to the executive airport on the west side, Ben asked, "Looking forward to getting home?"

"You bet I am," Marla answered, holding Danielle in her arms, "and I hope Jo providing this car and another plane ride is my last surprise for a long, long time." Noticing that Ben's expression changed after hearing her answer, she asked, "Why are you smiling?"

"I didn't realize I was. Just happy, I guess. Say Marla, who's your favorite country music singer?"

13

The days passed quickly, and it was the first day of September. Sitting in her living room, looking out on a bright, sunny morning, Marla acted on Jo's request to call her after she'd gotten settled back in. She shared with Jo her decision not to return to the university since it would mean entrusting Danielle's care to others, and that was something she couldn't contemplate.

"I understand completely, and I want you to know you and your family have been in my thoughts and prayers since Indianapolis," Jo said. "Marla, I know it's not a high priority for you now, but please let me know when you've had an opportunity to read a portion of my journals. Assuming you still have an interest, that is."

"I haven't read a portion, Jo. After we got back from Indianapolis, I read them all."

Growing up, Marla had dreamed of falling in love, getting married, and having a family. Those dreams had come true, but not flawlessly. She'd also dreamed of becoming a successful published author, and her three failed attempts weighed heavily. Although she had never said anything to anyone, she envied her husband's success. A collaboration with Jo just might make that dream come true.

"And do you still think turning them into a book is worth the investment of your time, and mine?"

"I do. I've already begun an outline, several of them actually. It's been a form of therapy to help me get over the scare with Danielle."

"Well, I honestly didn't expect that. But if you're willing, then so am I. With the understanding either of us can back out at any time without any hurt feelings by the other. Does that sound fair?"

"It does. As I was reading, I was hoping, even praying, for this call. This is wonderful!"

"Marla, I have people coming into my office for a meeting. I'm sorry to cut our call short. Can you call me tomorrow morning at nine so we can continue?"

◆ ◆ ◆

Weeks before committing to Marla, Jo had called Jennings to learn more about why he'd turned Ben down. Hearing his explanation, she had told him she would also say no, for much the same reasons.

He surprised her with his answer. "Jo, I encourage you to re-consider."

"Why?"

"Because your success, the story of your life, is unique. It can inspire others, whereas mine won't." He sensed her confusion and added, "I'm a white man who inherited an already successful family business. Sure, I grew the company significantly, but few people can relate to my story. And likely none will be inspired. But *you,* you're different."

"Because of my skin color, or my gender?"

"Both. And more. Much more. You began with nothing. Everything you have, everything you've accomplished, is solely attributable to you. Now *that's* an inspiring story. One worth telling."

"What does The Judge think?" she asked.

"We've known each other since we were tiny tots seeing who could pee the farthest in the backyard. But never once have I spoken for him. Why don't you give him a call?"

"I will. Jennings, I've tried to never envy others for what they have, but at this moment it's difficult."

"What do I have that you could possibly envy?"

"It's not you I envy. It's Lucy Mae."

"Why?"

"Because she has *you*, and those wonderful years with you. Growing up, I hoped my mother would find a man to love, to share her life, to grow old with. Like you and Lucy Mae. I don't know why, but it never happened for her. Maybe it was because I was part of the package."

"Jo, don't think that for a moment. Your mother made her choices, and you've made yours. We all miss Barrey, and I think he loved you as much as any man could love a woman."

The mention of Barrey Kelly's name caught her off guard, and she couldn't think of anything to say to keep up her end of the conversation. Thankfully, Jennings sensed it and came to her rescue.

"You know, if Lucy Mae weren't in the picture, and I were twenty years younger, or you were twenty years older, things might have been different between us."

"Mr. Eldridge, how you *can* charm a woman. I'm flattered, and I know you're only teasing me."

"I am. But given the times we've lived in, it would certainly have made our lives much more interesting. I love you as if you were my own daughter. I hope you know that."

"You know I do. I've told you so a thousand times."

"Are you going to call The Judge about the book idea?"

With practiced smoothness, Jennings had effortlessly changed the subject so they could move on. They continued talking for several minutes, and as they were ending, Jennings told her that if being married was her dream, then she should consider praying for that specific outcome. He reminded her they each had created journals for times like this, and she should look to hers for encouragement.

After saying their good-byes, Jo placed a call to The Judge's Frankfort office. She expected to leave a message, and was pleasantly surprised when the receptionist asked if she wanted to hold for a minute while The Judge finished another call.

After quickly recounting the book discussions, first with Marla and Ben, and then Jennings, she asked what he thought.

"Jo, I agree with Jennings. I haven't read his journals, or yours, but I do think your story, and the journals that helped carry you along your journey, can inspire others. And not just women. M n can learn a lot from you. I certainly have."

"Did you and Jennings take the same courses in Southern flattery? What could you, Mr. Chief Justice, have possibly learned from me?"

"My dear Josephine, I could write a book. Things I've wanted to say over the years, just never have. Which is why I'd like to see one written. And Marla will be wonderful to work with. If you decide to go ahead, that is."

14

Later that afternoon, sitting in her office, Jo reflected on what she'd agreed to in the call with Marla earlier that day. She'd read enough biographies to know you can't skip over a person's childhood. Or just focus only on the *ups* and ignore the *downs*. Like everyone, her *downs* were painful, often extremely painful, and she didn't know if she was prepared for the kind of sharing Marla was anticipating. That was why Jo had proposed the mutual escape clause, and was glad Marla had agreed. But for Jo, one thing was certain. There would be no discussion of Barrey Kelly.

Just thinking about Barrey caused the walls of her office to begin closing in on her, so Jo picked up her coat and headed for one of two exit doors at the back of the building. The sun was shining, the temperature mild – a perfect day for her to walk around the sprawling campus of the company she founded. As she walked, she turned her mind back in time to January, 2000.

◆ ◆ ◆

Jo had been so wrapped up in her career, first with Jennings' company and then her own, that a social life had always been pushed to the bottom of her priorities. Her work schedule, including the constant travel, and always being accompanied by a bodyguard, made meeting people especially challenging. She'd had one horrible relationship misfire a few years earlier, and she wasn't even looking, which made it such a surprise when "the one" entered her life.

Jo met Barrey Kelley when he became a new member of her church. Actually, he met *her* because he was the one who initiated the contact, approaching her one Sunday morning after the late service ended. She was five-ten, and had always been drawn, as she guessed most women were, to taller men. Barrey was an inch shorter, but the way he stood and carried himself told her he was no stranger to fitness centers. If not currently, then certainly in the past. His almost flawless complexion was darker than hers, but then she was lighter than most African-Americans. And he was handsome. Was he ever!

He invited her for coffee, and they agreed to meet one afternoon later in the week at a Starbucks near a place they both occasionally visited. As Jo would learn later, his visits to *that* place were becoming increasingly frequent.

As they got to know each other, Barrey's shortness of stature became inconsequential. She was drawn to his intellect, his shyness, and his sense of humor. He was a wonderful conversationalist, and listener, with a knack for making others feel completely at ease.

Jo's travel, and responsibilities growing and managing her company, made it difficult for them to be together. But over time, afternoon coffee turned into dinners, and an occasional movie or concert. They held hands, kissed, and were affectionate with each other. He didn't press for physical intimacy, something she initially appreciated, but began wondering about as their relationship entered its fifth month. Before she could find a way to broach the subject, a chance encounter led to the answer.

They ran into each other at a hospital in Lexington, near where they had their first coffee date. She was there to see her mother, who was actively dying. She was unaware of that term until she heard it used by one nurse to another to describe the condition of a patient. She found it initially off-putting, but then accepted it as an accurate description of her mother's condition.

Barrey's surprised expression when he saw her was more than she would have expected under the circumstances.

"Hi, Jo," he finally said, hesitantly. "What brings you here?"

"I was visiting my mother."

"Does she work here?"   •

"No, she's a patient. What brings you here?"

Again, he hesitated, saying, "Do you have time for coffee?"

She really needed to get back to the office, but didn't want to be rude. And she was curious about not receiving an answer to what she thought was a simple question. It was a warm spring day, so they took their coffees outside, sitting on a bench in a public area opposite the Starbucks. Her bodyguard was nearby, but no one would have made the connection.

Slightly hunched over, looking down at the cup held in both of his hands, he said, "Jo, I'm also a patient. Something I've wanted to tell you. Just haven't found the right time, or the right way." Then sitting up, he turned to face her, and said, "But I'm not going to make up a lie about why I'm here. So I guess this is the time."

"You don't have to tell me anything you aren't comfortable sharing," she answered, "except that I'm now concerned about you."

"I have complications of sickle-cell anemia. Do you know what that is?"

More than he could possibly imagine. She'd learned of her mother's own SCA diagnosis when she was still in elementary school, and had begun researching it then, keeping up with every new development over the years. In the United States, it almost always affects African-Americans.

Those infected with the malady don't die from it, but from complications. Like blood chronically low on oxygen, which can so severely damage nerves and organs, primarily kidneys, liver and spleen, as to be fatal. SCA can also cause blindness. Jo's mother was now both blind and in late-stage kidney failure.

"Jo, I'm so sorry to hear about your mother," Barrey said, following her disclosure.

"Thank you. That's very kind. She's not going to be with us long. But what about you?"

"I have complications. Nothing I want to go into sitting here now. Can we talk about it another time?"

"Of course, we can. And Barrey, I understand. Believe me, I do."

They had a dinner date already scheduled for the next evening, and it was then he told her. His illness had advanced to the point of doctors giving him his anticipated lifespan – less than two years. He told her he was certain she would want to end their relationship now that she knew, and he would understand.

Barrey was wrong about Jo's reaction, and his doctors were wrong about their prognosis.

Not only did they continue to see each other, they got married. After she proposed to him. Not out of sympathy, but because she'd fallen in love with him. Later, he credited their love and marriage for adding another year to his life. But their marriage was intentionally childless because Jo also had sickle-cell anemia, and its presence in both of them created two risks she and Barrey were not willing to accept – that the disease would be transferred to their child, and that their child would become an orphan with their knowledge.

Their marriage license, and later his death certificate, recorded the different spelling of his first name. The "e" was on his birth certificate, and despite his mother's unhappiness over the careless error of a hospital clerk, Barrey proudly accepted it as soon as he learned to spell. He thought it made him different from other children. As far as Jo was concerned, it was the only less-than-perfect thing about him.

A few days after he accepted her proposal, Barrey gave Jo a Tiffany gold charm bracelet. He told her she would be getting a charm on at least three occasions every year, her birthday, Valentine's Day and

Christmas, reserving, he said, the right for others on special occasions. Or no occasions, just whenever he wanted.

He lived long enough to give her nine in addition to the heart with *Jo* engraved on it that came with the bracelet. All gold. A horse, symbolizing their shared love for Kentucky. A Jerusalem cross, inspired by one they saw at the National Cathedral in Washington, D.C. A circle with her mother's name and birthdate engraved. And others given in remembrance of something special between them. The last one, like the first, was a heart, with *Forever* engraved.

Although *forever* for them would be cruelly cut short, his symptoms were manageable, and he didn't suffer very much. They had been cautiously optimistic they would beat the odds, defy the medical experts. He told her soon after she learned of his prognosis that he wanted to live to see the new millennium. He died of heart failure at home, in his sleep, lying next to her, on January 11th, 2000. It was three years and one month after he introduced himself at church.

A few days earlier, Barrey must have experienced a premonition because he told her he'd decided to greet each new day by reciting a Native American expression he'd just read. They were sitting outside on the patio, bundled up, savoring the setting winter sun. Despite his pronounced weight loss, and overall weakened condition, he was, in her eyes, the same beautiful man she first laid eyes on.

"Don't you mean *African* American?" she asked.

"No. I was reading about a famous chief, don't recall the tribe, who inspired his braves about to enter combat by saying, 'Today is a good day to die.'" When she didn't respond, he added, "The expression *live each day as if it was my last* never made sense to me. No one is going to do that."

She sensed there was more he wanted to say, so she silently encouraged him to continue. What he said gave her direction for the rest of her life.

"You see, Jo, a few days after I was diagnosed, and knew my time was limited, I lifted the burden up in prayer. That prayer was answered."

"In what way?"

"The next day, this thought entered my mind – to live each day so that if it *were* my last, I would be proud of how I conducted myself. What I said. What I did. How I treated others."

She reached over with her right hand, taking his left in hers and squeezing it. The look he gave her conveyed unconditional love, and she hoped hers did, as well. The last words they spoke to each other every night of their marriage were "I love you." Three nights later, they *were* the last words.

Jo shivered in the cold as she held hands with The Judge and Jennings, their presence on each side of her comforting and their silence welcomed. Nothing they could say would change how she felt, and they knew it. Jo knew it would end the way it did, but when the day actually came, she felt devastated. And who's ever fully prepared to say good-bye in a way that has such visual finality? Responding to her request, Jennings said a short prayer before they left Barrey's grave and made their way back down the gently sloping incline to the car where her driver waited.

As they drove away, Jo thanked God for bringing Barrey into her life, and told Him she would be content if he was not only "the one", but the *only* one. What they had together was so special, she doubted it could ever happen again. That night, alone in their bed, Jo prayed for the strength to endure a future without Barrey.

◆ ◆ ◆

The sun was setting, so Jo headed back to her office building, raising her collar against a chilly breeze that had come up. And she certainly hadn't warmed herself with her afternoon walk down memory lane.

In a few months, at her own initiation, the life she had known for several decades would come to an end. She would no longer be one of the most powerful and influential people in Kentucky, and she didn't even have a plan for how she was going to spend her days after the first of the year. Uncharacteristically, despite her phenomenal wealth, she began focusing on what she'd wanted in life that would forever be out of her reach. Children of her own. Marriage to a man she'd loved for decades. And time.

15

"Marla, do you still believe it's absolutely necessary to identify me in this book?"

As Jo had requested the day before, Marla called her precisely at nine the next morning. Sitting at the kitchen table, she had a legal pad and a pen ready to record notes of the coming conversation.

"I don't think it works any other way," Marla answered. "Readers will have to know about you to give credibility to your thoughts, and the words of others that have inspired you."

"You said you'd worked up some outlines. Can you share what you're thinking?"

"Sure. The overall perspective of your journals is that of a woman, more particularly, a woman of color.

"Isn't that a pretty easy conclusion to reach? What else?"

"Well, I'm not very familiar with the genres, but intuitively I think most books in the self-help and inspirational categories, and the biographies and autobiographies of successful people, have been either written by or about a white man."

"Marla, I'm impressed. Since I *do* read those books, I can assure you that your intuition is absolutely on target. And I'm not being judgmental about either race or gender – it's simply a reality. But what does it mean to *us?*"

"It means our book will be different. Hopefully, dramatically different."

"I'm with you. Here's another thought. You might want to carefully review all the books you can find written in the last year about the challenges women face in the workplace, such as hiring, pay and advancement."

"Okay. What am I looking for?" Marla asked.

"Solutions."

"Solutions?"

"Yes. Marla, it's easy to write about problems. To document them empirically. It's much harder to come up with solutions. If you agree, let's make our focus, or at least one of them, gender inequality. It's the sun around which so many other women's issues orbit. In a manner of speaking."

"I agree. This is great!" Marla said, looking at her notes. "I'm so excited you agreed to go ahead."

"Let's plan on talking again in a couple of weeks. By then, we'll both have had time to give it a lot more thought."

Jo traveled to Bowling Green three weeks later for an ESOP-related meeting with Ben and Jennings, and met with Marla at her house later in the day. It was an unseasonably warm first week in October, so they made themselves comfortable on the rooftop deck. Jo had skillfully balanced a bottle of Chardonnay and two wine glasses in one hand, her well-worn soft leather briefcase in the other. Danielle was awake as Marla carried her up the stairs, but remained quiet when tucked into her cradle.

"Marla, you know so much about me. May we begin today with you telling me *your* story?"

Because of Ben's first meeting with Jo, Marla had anticipated this moment, and was prepared.

"Well, I was born in Australia. I'm an only child, and as a young girl, my father was recruited to teach at Western, so I was educated in Bowling Green all the way through university graduation. After that, I joined the Peace Corps and went to Indonesia."

"What did you do there?"

"I worked with at-risk children, an interest you and I have in common. On my first R&R break, I went to visit my birth country and met the man who would become my husband."

She went on to tell Jo about Daniel, and the circumstances of his death.

"How tragic. Marla, I'm so sorry. Is your family here, or back in Australia?"

"Ben's family is my family. My parents are both deceased, and I have no brothers or sisters."

"And is little Danielle named after Daniel?"

This lady misses nothing, Marla thought. She confirmed Jo's guess, and shared details of Ben's obsession before meeting her with having a son to carry on his family name. But she didn't tell her about his son Bartolome. If this were ever disclosed, it would need to come from Ben.

"You already know about my career as a university professor, professional writing coach and published author. Oh, and of course," she said, looking down at Danielle, "mother. Since you know how Ben and I met, I guess that's my story."

Eager to move on, Marla turned the conversation toward her guest. "I know your relationship with Ben's father and Jennings goes all the way back to when you were born. But how did your mother meet them?"

"Now that's a story I'd be delighted to tell. One I anticipated."

Jo reached for her briefcase, opened it, and withdrew a large brown envelope. She handled it with such gentleness Marla assumed it had to be something of great value, or significance. Jo opened it and handed Marla a carefully preserved, professional-looking black and white photo, perhaps taken by a newspaper photographer.

"Do you recognize anyone?" Jo asked.

"That's Martin Luther King," Marla blurted out, pointing to the man in the center of the picture, arms locked with four other people, standing in front of a modest red brick church. "Who are the others?" Marla asked, focused on three young men, one black and two white, and one black woman. "They all look so young. Who's the woman?"

"They were all teenagers at the time," Jo answered. "The woman is my mother."

"Your mother? She's so beautiful! And the men? They're all so handsome. Do you think your mother knew any of them? She must have."

"I can tell you she certainly knew one of them better than the others. This is the only picture I have of my father. He's the one to her immediate left. They'd just met the night before, and I'm the happy result. Those things happened even back then. Mother said he left to go back to college up North a few hours after this picture was taken. He never knew about me."

"This is fascinating. But how does it connect your mother to Ben's father and Jennings? Wait! Are they the other two men in the picture?"

"They are," Jo answered, smiling.

"*They* were Freedom Riders?" Marla exclaimed, understanding the implication.

"They were. Privileged white boys who risked their lives for a cause they believed in. Jennings carried his beliefs into the business world, Ben's father carried them into the courtroom. But it wouldn't surprise me if their children don't know. It would be uncharacteristic for either one to talk about their heroics during that long-ago summer."

"Jo, I honestly don't think Ben knows. Or if he does, he's never said anything to me. And I certainly won't say anything. How did you get the picture?"

"A friend of Jennings' father owned the local newspaper. It came across what was called the wire service at the time, a compilation of the day's available photos for putting in the paper. He recognized Jennings and called his father, giving him the courtesy of keeping it out of the paper."

"What did his father say?"

"Print the damn picture! I'm proud of my son, and that Taylor boy, too."

"Did they put it in the paper?" Marla asked

"No. Don't know why. But they gave the picture to Jennings' father, and he had copies made. That's how Mother got hers."

Marla thought about all the pictures she had from the years she had with her father, and felt sorry for Jo.

"So you see, Marla, I never knew the man responsible for me being here. But all my life I've been blessed with the love and caring of those two remarkable men. Neither tried to be a father figure. That wouldn't have been appropriate. If things had been different, maybe things would have been different."

Marla didn't know what to make of her last sentence, but before she could ask, Danielle began crying. As Marla reached for the diaper bag, Jo said, "I've done a lot of things in my life, but never once changed a baby's diaper. Are you up to giving instruction to a first-timer?"

Since Danielle wasn't "muddy", it wasn't an unpleasant experience. As they were finishing up, Jo said, "This has been so unlike me, Marla. Talking so much. And especially about me."

"I'm glad you did. There's much I need to understand, so I can put *your* voice on paper to share with others. Jo, I was wondering, are you as enthusiastic as I am?"

"No."

16

Jo's answer with a tape recorder now running startled Marla. Was the project over before it had begun? Before Marla could recover, Jo elaborated on her one-word answer while refilling their wine glasses.

"Marla, it's a given I've been successful in business. It's what I set out to achieve. It's what I dreamed about ever since I was a little girl." She stopped, but Marla remained silent. "We both know Jennings turned Ben down. I'm not offended that I'm your Plan B, but Jennings and I talked, and I now have some of his doubts. Neither of us sees ourselves as role models for others, and we share the same concern about privacy. It's not who we are."

"But when you called saying you were going ahead, you told me it was partly because Jennings had encouraged you. So I guess I don't understand."

"Do you know the Statler Brothers?" Jo asked, seemingly out of the blue.

"Of course. I'm a country music fan."

"Then you may remember in one of their songs they sing about having a gimmick like Charley Pride has."

"Charley Pride? Oh, I think I get it. He's a black artist in an almost entirely white industry. Is that what Jennings meant?"

"It is. That I'm a woman in a country in which business, industry, government – it's an endless list – is dominated by men."

"Jo, with all due respect to a man we both admire, I wouldn't characterize you as a gimmick. I do believe what's in your journals will be inspirational to others, and it *is* the fact that you are a woman, a woman of color, that accounts for a lot of my enthusiasm."

"You said something earlier about this being a dream come true for you. What did you mean?"

"My dream is to be a successful published author, and I'm 'O' for three. It's my profession, and okay, it pisses me off that my husband, with no training but with *my* coaching and editing, has a New York Times bestseller his first time." Marla had finally articulated a feeling she'd never shared with anyone.

"Marla, I don't share your enthusiasm that my journals have the makings of a bestseller, but I'll do all I can to help. If it doesn't happen with me, and it probably won't, then let's pray together that something else will come along that'll get you that dream."

Marla couldn't say anything for a moment. She was deeply moved that Jo got it – that she truly understood how Marla felt. As Marla struggled to keep her composure, Jo stepped in to help.

"First things first. Let's pause while you rewind your tape and erase that comment about Danielle's father."

"Oh, my God! Thank you! I don't even want to think about what would happen if Ben heard what I said. And that I said it to you."

Once the erasing was complete, Jo continued. "With our enthusiasm differences now on record, my participation comes with some ground rules. Ready?" Marla nodded. "I understand, and for now accept, that I must be identified in order to give the book credibility. But it must not be *about* me."

"I don't understand the distinction," Marla interrupted.

"To me, it's a very clear one. Our approach must be about inspiring readers, assuming we have any, not to admire and attempt to emulate me. I see it as encouraging them to take control of their own lives, and chart their own course."

"That's not what I was thinking, so let me make certain I understand. Instead of this being a book about how your journals helped *you* achieve your success, you want it to be focused on the *reader?*"

"Yes. Instead of someone just reading books about other people, about success principals this author or that author deems important, why not encourage readers to create their own book? What *they* aspire to, what *they* think of in terms of success and, more importantly, happiness. And it will be more valuable to them, and hopefully, more enduring, because *they* wrote it."

"Jo, in all your reading, have you ever seen this approach before?"

"No, I haven't. Doesn't mean other such books don't exist, I'm just not aware of any. Marla, this is precisely what Jennings and I did for ourselves. And isn't this what was intriguing, first to Ben, and then you?"

"You're absolutely right. We'll be encouraging readers to become keepers of their own journals. That's great! Let's keep going. You said 'conditions.' What else?"

"Brevity. I've never written a book, but for one like this, I don't see why you, we, can't avoid saying in pages what can be said in paragraphs. Or avoiding paragraphs when a sentence or two will suffice. As I heard Jennings once say about a politician, 'There was no need for him to float a battleship of words around a row boat of thought.'"

Laughing, Marla added, "That could be challenging, but duly noted. What else?"

"Not a condition, rather my commitment that I won't get our roles confused. You're the writer, and a fine one. I'm a resource. Just tell me what you need."

"Thank you for the kind words," Marla said, "but you're taking a leap of faith. All you have is my assurance that I'm qualified to collaborate with you."

"Marla, I read all three of your books, and thoroughly enjoyed them. You're a wonderful writer. If anyone can make something good out of my clumsy journals, it's you."

"Jo, I don't know what to say. Other than I'm surprised, and flattered by your kind words."

"So here's a question. When you read my journals, did you find the content to be gender, age or profession-specific?"

"I wasn't looking for that as I read," Marla answered, "but now that you mention it, no, I didn't."

"Okay. You said you were overwhelmed by both the volume and the content of the journals. So wouldn't it make sense for us to begin a narrowing process?" Marla nodded and Jo continued. "Let's take incremental steps, beginning with selecting a target audience. Since you insist on revealing me, doesn't it stand to reason that women are far more likely to be inspired by my story than men would be?"

"It does. I'll begin organizing the journal entries in different formats, creating various storylines for you to consider. Now that we have our audience in mind, it'll be easier to focus on message and tone. And that, as we agreed, will be *my* job."

"I'm going to have to leave soon, but before I do, have you identified specific topics you think should be addressed?"

"I have," Marla answered, flipping through her notebook and finding the page she was looking for. "Five. The biggest one is workplace barriers to equality of opportunity and condition."

"Sounds good," Jo said, in an encouraging tone. "Go on."

"Income disparity between men and women doing the same work."

"Okay."

"Sexual harassment. At work. College campuses. Everywhere. The fourth is the lack of women in positions of authority in government, as well as in executive suites and boardrooms."

"And the fifth?"

"Glass ceilings."

"Okay. What about glass cliffs?"

"I've never heard that term," Marla answered.

"Just write it down next to glass ceilings," Jo said, "and we'll discuss it later. One more thing. We need to be careful not to overstate problems and issues, and to separate perception from reality. We'll address what's real, not what's imagined."

"I agree completely," Marla said, understanding their meeting had ended. She enjoyed her time with Jo so much, she hated for it to come to an end, so she impulsively asked, "Jo, do you have plans for Thanksgiving? I know it's only a few weeks away, and you probably do. But if you don't, we'd love to have you join us. The 'us' will be Ben and me, The Judge, and Jennings and Lucy Mae. Oh, and Beverly. Any chance you can join us?"

"It's very sweet of you to ask. I do have plans, but they can change if I can come as a package."

"How so?"

"As you know, I'm never without security. Only one of the men, Charles Flener, has grown children living away who don't come back to Kentucky for Thanksgiving. I invited Charlie and his wife Ruth to be with me for a quiet dinner. I don't want to be a burden in accepting, but it would need to be a threesome. And I'm guessing you invited me without checking with Ben first."

"You're right, but I know Ben and everyone else would love to have you. You haven't seen it, but we have a three-bedroom guest suite downstairs, so we can all be together. Including the Fleners."

As Marla walked Jo to the front door, she asked, "Jo, would it be okay if I talked with Ben from time to time about the book. He's been very successful in business, he's certainly had his own personal and professional challenges, and he's an excellent writer in his own right. And I think a male perspective would be valuable."

"I think that's an excellent suggestion. Of course."

As Marla opened the door, she summoned the courage to ask a final question. "Would you mind if I also talked with Jennings and The Judge? For the same reason as Ben. And because they know you so well."

The long silence worried Marla. Had she overstepped the boundaries of both a book collaboration and a new friendship?

Finally, Jo said while hugging Marla, "Talking with them will be fine with me, although it may not be something *they'll* want to do."

After Jo left, Marla realized the woman had totally captivated her. And the potential opportunity to peel back a layer or two by talking with Jennings and The Judge, guarded as they might be, energized her thinking as she awaited Ben's arrival home. But there was something else occupying Marla's thoughts. Jo's appearance.

17

That evening, as Marla anticipated, Ben asked about her meeting with Jo, and he listened attentively as she recounted the details of their discussion. When she finished, he said, "Marla, I'm delighted for you, and for Jo. And I've been thinking about something else you've probably already thought of."

"What?"

"Well, I understand your decision about not returning to WKU because of Danielle, but does it have to be all or nothing? By that I mean, is there any reason why you can't reactivate your coaching and editing as your own business, working with other authors? You could take on as much or as little as you want, and when you want."

Marla was touched, even a little flabbergasted, by Ben's thoughtfulness. "I hadn't been thinking that way, Ben. I was so focused on Danielle and the project with Jo. If I do, and I'm certain I will, are you okay with writers coming here to the house from time to time? It's the only way I see it being workable."

"No problem at all. But you may be happier with a physical separation of home and business. There's an empty office in the foundation's space on the first floor, and you and your clients would have access to the kitchen and the rest-rooms. Only an elevator ride away for you and Danielle."

"What a wonderful solution! Ben, I don't know how to thank you," she said, hugging him as they sat on the living room sofa.

"Something will occur to you," he answered, smiling. "And before we get distracted, I have news of my own. A decision I think will please you." Her nod and smile invited him to continue. "I'm not going to pursue politics. The thing with Danielle scared both of us, and even if it's all behind us as we've been told it is, I'm not going to do anything that will take me away from the two of you."

"Ben, you knew I'd be delighted, and I am," she said, hugging and kissing him. "Have you decided what you're going to do when Jennings leaves the company?"

"We have plenty of money, so that's not a worry. Finish my sequel, hopefully with your help. Be involved with the foundation, if I'm needed there. And…maybe…"

"Ben, it's not like you to be at a loss for words. What?"

"Well, it sort of involves you. I was thinking …maybe a sibling for Danielle."

"You think it *sort of* involves me?" Marla exclaimed, laughing.

"Okay, poor choice of words. But you get my drift."

Taking his hand in hers, she said, "And *you* consider yourself a wordsmith. What say we *drift* on upstairs?"

Later, as they lay intertwined in bed, Marla remembered to tell Ben about the Thanksgiving invitation to Jo and the Fleners. He hugged her and added he only wished he'd thought of it.

"Marla, you said you wanted to talk with Dad about the book. He called earlier today to say he was going to be in town over the weekend."

Ben had a Saturday morning meeting at the office with Jennings, so Marla invited The Judge to join her for coffee at their residence one floor above his. The Judge arrived right on time, and soon found himself in the living room rocking chair, his granddaughter sleeping in his arms.

Marla knew The Judge's practice of almost always wearing a suit and tie in public was a combination of both what he thought people expected, as well as his desire to always look his best. But when he *could* relax, he chose casual slacks and whatever the weather would suggest. For this meeting, he wore a tan cashmere sweater over a starched blue button-down collar shirt, and tasseled brown loafers.

"Marla, I'm so looking forward to January, when you and I'll have more time to spend just like this."

"Me, too. Judge, I'm always happy when we're together, but I had an ulterior motive in inviting you this morning. I hope you won't be upset with me."

"Upset with you? Never. What's on your mind?"

Marla replayed the update she'd given Ben a few days earlier, ending with Jo giving permission for her to talk with The Judge and Jennings.

"What can we tell you that Jo can't?" The Judge asked.

"I don't know. There's so much I want to know, need to know, about Jo to help her with the book. More insight into her as a person, as well as her life and career. She's reluctant to talk about herself."

"I understand, and I'm happy to help. If I can. How will this work?"

Marla told The Judge she wanted to ask him about Jo's life away from her work, and that Jo had given her permission to record conversations with her. As she was setting up the recorder, The Judge said he didn't mind being recorded, but insisted that Marla get Jo's approval. Marla made the call from the kitchen phone, and although initially hesitant, Jo agreed.

"Jo and I talked about her first few years until she started school. Maybe you could start there."

"Okay. Anyone who knows her will tell you her mother was the greatest influence in her life. Although Cynthia only graduated high school, she was very bright and very well read. Jo will tell you it was her mother who instilled in her a love of learning, and to being the best she could possibly be at whatever she did."

"Judge, I should tell you she showed me the picture, so I know about the Freedom Riders, and the father she never knew."

"Now that's something I'm *not* going to talk about. Jennings and I did what we did, and never saw a need to talk about it. Our children don't know, and I'm asking you, as will Jennings, to respect our wishes. And if there's any chance Ben will hear this tape, we need to start over."

"I haven't said anything to Ben, and I won't. I promised the same thing to Jo. I just wanted you to know I know."

"Understood. Back to Jo. She was an outstanding student, and got what we called a *full ride* scholarship to Western. Both she and her mother were happy because they could continue living together while she got her degree."

"Was the scholarship just academic? Or did she also excel at sports? I would think she did since she's such an over-achiever in every other way."

The Judge hesitated longer than Marla thought the question merited, then said, "I think that's something best left for you to discuss with Jo."

Surprised, and disappointed, Marla kept going, asking just about academics.

"She graduated near the top of her class. She was a business major. No surprise there, I guess."

"Not at all. What about after graduation?"

"That will be Jennings' area. She went to work for one of his companies."

"Got it. Since you know the premise of our book, can you tell me about challenges she faced as a woman, and how she dealt with them?"

Although his expression didn't change, his body language did. Marla noticed a stiffening in his posture, and that he was no longer as relaxed as when they'd begun the conversation. "Now we're getting into an uncomfortable area," he finally said. "And aren't these things you should be asking Jo?"

"I will. I'm just worried her modesty will keep us from sharing things in the book that would be so helpful to other women. Things like how she dealt with discrimination. Sexual harassment. If she had those issues, that is."

"Marla, I'm not going tell you anything I think must come from her, but I will tell you this. Josephine Gilpin is a beautiful woman, and it would be foolish for anyone to think she somehow escaped those problems. There's a reason she has round-the-clock security."

"I thought the bodyguards were protecting her as the company's leader. And that they'd be there if the CEO was a man. Were there other problems?"

The Judge looked at her, but didn't answer for several moments. "Marla, like all of us, Jo's had her challenges, and has been shaped by the world around her. Things happened that shouldn't have, and I doubt she'll talk with you about them. What I *can* tell you is that I admire her more than any person, man or woman, I've ever known."

Given all the people he would have encountered during his high-profile career, such an accolade further reinforced how remarkable Jo was. And it even further energized Marla about working on what she regarded as a *must do* project.

"She seems to be just about perfect, wouldn't you say?"

"No, I wouldn't. Jo's not perfect. Not even close. None of us are, and I would say that if she were sitting here. I guess in a way, she is." The Judge was looking at the recorder.

"I agree, Judge. I just got carried away, hearing how much you admire her."

"I couldn't be prouder of her, what she's accomplished, the person she became. But I was always careful to maintain a respectful distance."

Marla understood the first sentence of his answer, but not the second. Why would he feel the need to maintain distance from her? And he said a "respectful" distance, as if he could ever be anything *but* respectful to others. She was about to ask a follow-up question when Ben arrived home, signaling their need to leave for their lunch reservation.

Jennings had agreed to meet with Marla the next afternoon, after he and Lucy Mae had had their lunch following church. For all their wealth, Lucy Mae and Jennings lived in a home only slightly less modest than Jo's, built while they were raising their children and anticipating grandchildren.

Marla was pleased that Jennings seemed happy to talk about Jo's career, with obvious pride in her achievements. Sitting out on his sun porch, sharing a pitcher of iced tea with her, he told of offering Jo a high profile entry-level management position in one of his companies after she graduated from college. He said it was a job virtually assuring her of a rapid rise within the organization, but she turned him down.

"Why?"

"She asked for an outside sales position, one in which much of her compensation would be tied directly to her performance. To her ability to close sales." He went on to explain that while she excelled at sales in his company through hard work and discipline, she wasn't shy in telling him her real dream was to someday own her own company."

"How did she get from working for you to owning her own company?"

"One day she came to me with a detailed business plan to create a company to manufacture cosmetics for women of color. Sounded like a good idea to me, and she was very passionate, so I offered her a small loan to get started. She paid it back quickly, and I helped her get her own bank financing. She was self-sufficient within her first year, and we all know what she's achieved since then."

Like The Judge, Jennings understood the basics of the book Marla was helping Jo write, so he provided numerous anecdotal stories about her surviving economic downturns, changing markets, a poorly-timed acquisition, even a palace coup.

"Palace coup. Now *that* sounds interesting," Marla said.

"Details must come from Jo. It involved a conspiracy of members of her executive team, in collusion with some of her lenders and one of her competitors, trying to gain control of her company."

"What happened?" Marla asked, realizing how tame her professional challenges had been compared to those Jo had encountered.

"They underestimated Jo – and failed miserably."

"It's a world I don't understand, that's for sure. Jennings, I have just one more question. What do you think was the most memorable leadership thing Jo ever did?"

"That's an easy one. September 11th."

"9-11?"

"I never liked the abbreviation, but yes. Jo was three time zones behind New York, watching on television in her hotel room. By early afternoon, she'd arranged a conference call with all her executives, those in Versailles and those who were also travelling. She told them no one knew what it meant for the country, for the world, but one thing she did know. None of her employees would lose their job, and seeing to *that* was the responsibility of every man and woman on the call."

"What leadership! And you did say there were women on the call. So some of her top executives back then were women?"

"Of course, they were. Not because they were woman. But because they were women qualified for the positions they occupied. It's always been that way with Jo, from the very beginning."

Marla thanked Jennings for his time and his sharing about Jo, and on the way out apologized to Lucy Mae for taking her husband away from her on a Sunday afternoon.

As Marla drove away, she reflected on her two interviews. The subject had been Jo Gilpin, but there was something different in how the two men regarded her. She couldn't put her finger on anything specific either of them said, or didn't say, but there was something there, just like she'd suggested to Ben over dinner at the Hyatt just a few weeks ago.

18

"Judge, how nice to hear your voice. I was just thinking about you."
It was late afternoon, and Jo was in her office. And she *had* been
thinking about both The Judge and Jennings, wondering what they'd
shared with Marla that she would have preferred they hadn't. But she
trusted both men implicitly, and nothing would appear in a book
without her approval. If the book ever happened.

"Really? Why?" he asked.

"Oh, just wondering what you and Jennings told Marla about me.
You have spoken with her, haven't you?"

"You bet. Gave her all the sordid details. Most of them, anyway.
Jennings probably gave her the rest."

"I know you're only kidding, but in case you're not, I'll listen to
the tapes."

"Burned them. Marla has only her memory, and it will be her
word against ours."

Laughing, Jo said, "Now, why *did* you call?"

"To invite you to dinner."

Frankfort was only sixteen miles from Versailles, but they seldom
saw each other. What separated them was not geography, but their
respective calendars overflowing with professional commitments. Jo
often wished it were otherwise and hoped The Judge did, as well.

"I'd love to! Here or there?"

Before he could answer, Jo continued by offering home cooking as
an alternative to restaurant fare – an offer he quickly accepted.

"What time shall I tell the gun-toting staff to expect a distinguished visitor?" she asked.

"I don't know who else you're inviting, but this undistinguished country lawyer can be there at seven."

"Judge, I don't intend to share you with anyone else. I'm so glad you called, and tomorrow evening can't come soon enough."

The Judge lived by the mantra *better never than late*, so shortly before seven the next evening he was standing in the foyer of Jo's home. They always greeted each other with a chaste kiss on the cheek, but tonight the hug that followed lasted longer, and was different. Or at least that's how Jo felt. Casting the thought aside, she took his hand and led him to the parlor where his favorite bourbon awaited.

Each time she saw him in a suit and tie, she was reminded of the actor Jimmy Stewart. The Judge was always impeccably dressed, whether the occasion was formal or casual. Tonight was just-after-work attire for both of them, with him in a chalk gray suit, white shirt and royal blue tie. Handkerchief carefully folded and peeking out of his jacket pocket.

Before leaving for the office that morning, Jo had pinned an antique gold broche on her pale blue St. John tweed jacket. The broche was simple in design but of immeasurable value since it had belonged to The Judge's mother. He'd given it to her one day for no special occasion – just because he'd said he wanted her to have it. Although one of her few indulgences was expensive watches, she'd selected a plain one given to her as a college graduation gift. He noticed both.

"My mother's broche couldn't be more beautifully displayed. Thank you for wearing it tonight. And isn't that the watch Jennings and I gave you?"

"It is. And I treasure it. And the broche, of course."

He lifted his glass toward hers as they stood by the fireplace, saying, "To a beautiful woman, and wonderful memories."

Their glasses, one containing bourbon and the other red wine, touched and created a sound only possible with the coming together of expensive crystal. Much as she loved this man, and Jennings, she'd never acquired their taste for what had made Kentucky famous.

"Thank you," Jo said. "Let's sit, or are you starving? Dinner's ready, waiting for us."

"If dinner can wait, let's chat for a while. I've always found this to be such a pleasant room."

As they sat side by side on the sofa, Jo said, "Tell the truth. Will there be any surprises if I listen to your conversation with Marla?"

"Don't think so. I didn't tell her much, and certainly nothing about your private life."

"I can't think of anything in my private life you could share that would've been a problem."

"So it would have been okay for me to tell her about how you dealt with one Winston Collins?"

"You know about that? How?"

"I won't say I know *all* about it. And I wasn't being serious. I'd never say anything, to anyone."

"I know you wouldn't. But how did *you* find out?"

"Jo, I've been interested in everything you've ever shared with me that was of interest to you. Jennings, too, but not in the same way. You told us about dating Winston, and mentioned him frequently. Then, all of a sudden, we never heard his name again. Or at least I didn't."

"Go on."

"Okay. He was a high profile political operative. Almost everyone elected in Kentucky, and that includes me, knew him, or *of* him. His career collapsed almost overnight, and it was about the same time you stopped making any mention of him. The ability to put one and one together has been very helpful to me when I sit in my black robes on my lofty perch."

"Why didn't you say anything?"

"I didn't *know* anything for certain. And I would have only said or done something if I thought it was necessary to keep you from getting hurt. Physically, that is. The rest was your business, and yours alone."

"What about his wife?" she asked.

"He had a wife?" The Judge asked, clearly surprised.

Jo confirmed what he had suspected about her hand in Winston's career difficulties, and she told him what he didn't know – about the lawyer wife who, because of Jo, became aware of Winston's infidelities. But without knowing the source.

"I can't say he didn't have it coming, and the way it happened had a rather elegant, and discrete, touch to it. Others might not have been as restrained as you."

"It wasn't my first thought, but Charlie wouldn't lend me his gun, or look for a rusty knife."

Lifting his glass, The Judge proposed another toast. "Here's to reason, and resourcefulness, prevailing over instinct, and weapons."

They sat silently, looking at each other, when Jo remembered something he'd said. It caused a strange feeling to overtake her, and if this was an opening, she wasn't about to let it pass by.

"Judge, a few minutes ago you said something I didn't understand." He nodded for her to continue.

"I don't remember the exact words, but it was something about you and Jennings always having an interest in things of interest to me, but in different ways. What did you mean?"

His hesitation before answering enhanced that strangely pleasant feeling in Jo. A few seconds seemed like an eternity.

"Jo," he answered, slowly, looking down at the bourbon glass in his hand, "I've only ever loved two women in my life." Then he looked up, and toward her, saying, "Ben's mother. And you."

"You and Jennings have told me you loved me since I was a little girl, and I've said the same thing to both of you. So I don't...." she stopped, unable to finish because at that moment she thought she *did* understand.

"I hadn't planned on having this conversation tonight," he said, "or ever, really." He then stood up, and walked over to the window to gather his thoughts. Turning around, he said, "Many people, my son foremost among them, have wondered why I never remarried after his mother died."

"You can now include me," she replied. "Especially since I can't imagine a more desirable husband candidate. Please don't say any more if you don't want to."

"Since my wife died, the only person I've ever loved in that way, the only person I would want to be married to....is you."

There it was. Feelings she'd had for this man for so long she now knew were shared.

"But she died so long ago," Jo said, as she struggled to put *her* words together. "Why've you never said anything?"

"That's a question Jennings has asked me a couple hundred times over the years."

"Jennings?"

"Couldn't go through life not talking with someone. And he's the only one I told."

Jo wanted to make it as easy as possible for him to take the conversation where she hoped they both wanted it to go.

"Jennings is just about the smartest man I know, well, tied with you. So why haven't you taken his advice, and said something?"

"Jo, you know why. It just wasn't possible."

"Maybe years ago. Certainly when I was married to Barrey. But Judge, it's 2016. Donald Trump is going to be president in a few months. *Anything* is possible!" The Judge didn't say anything as he returned to sit next to her on the sofa. "What I'm saying is something I've also wanted to say forever. My school-girl crush on a much older man turned into true love after I graduated from college. I never acted on it for what I think are the same reasons you didn't either. I let our age difference, and our ethnicity, trump my true feelings. Oh, my God! Did I just say *trump*? Please forgive me!"

Both of them laughed at her word choice, lightening the atmosphere at just the right moment.

"Jo, you're right. About the trumping. But I no longer care what anyone thinks. Except for one person." He paused, then added, "I remember you telling me you proposed to Barrey. Are you open to a role reversal?"

She nodded, her eyes becoming moist in anticipation of what his next words might be.

The Chief Justice of the Supreme Court of Kentucky, a man she had loved and admired all her life, set his glass on the floor and began to kneel in front of her. As he did, his knee gave way, he lost his balance, and went sprawling onto the floor. When he quickly scrambled to a standing position, straightening his suit coat, Jo's momentary concern that he might have injured himself gave way to laughter that caused her to unconsciously hug herself, rocking side-to-side.

He gave her a few moments to compose herself, then said, "Your expression of concern about my well-being is breathtaking." Then *he* began laughing.

As he sat back down beside her, she reached for his hand and said, "Sorry. Couldn't help myself. But really, did you hurt yourself?"

"Well, my dignity is bruised, but I think I'll recover. Now, where were we?"

"You fell down before I could say yes."

He pulled her up as he stood, and they kissed passionately. It was everything Jo had allowed herself to imagine when she'd dreamed about this moment for over thirty years. Her mother's words came rushing back to her. *Dreams never come true for those who never dream.*

Having dinner together had been the original plan for the evening. But eating wasn't what they both now wanted to do together.

Later, as she lay in his arms in her bedroom upstairs, reality intruded.

"I have a few questions," she said. "Three, actually."

"And I hope I have the right answers."

"When do you want to break the news to the folks in Bowling Green?"

"We'll all be together for Thanksgiving in a couple of weeks. Alright if we wait until then?"

"Sure."

"Good. What's the next question?"

"I've only known you as Judge. Now what? Benjamin? Ben?"

"Jo, as much as I've wanted us to be where we are right now, and not just physically, *that* thought never occurred to me. Do we have to decide tonight?"

"No, of course not," she answered, turning her head slightly away from him.

"And the last question?"

"When we tell Ben and Marla, are we also going to tell them about my SCA?"

19

Jo's overnight guest joined her in the kitchen, and together they resolved the name question over a pre-dawn breakfast. "Have a wonderful day, Judge," she said, kissing him good-bye as he departed for his Frankfort office and she headed for hers in Versailles.

A few days earlier, Jo had offered Ben a position on the board of her new foundation, not thinking about the potential problem of his holding positions on the board of both a benefactor and its intended recipient. It was a conflict she immediately understood, and one she was embarrassed she hadn't thought of. And when she jumped at Ben's suggestion of Marla, he'd asked her not to disclose the origin of the idea.

Jo waited until nine before calling Marla to make her the offer.

"Jo, I'm honored, and thrilled! I've never been on a board before, but I'm a quick-study, and you have my commitment to give you my very best."

"I know you will, and I'm delighted you've accepted. We're putting the documents together and planning our first meeting, so you'll be getting some information soon."

"I'll keep an eye out for it. Jo, I was planning on calling you anyway. Do you have a few more minutes to talk? Something just happened that's made all our lives more interesting than they already were."

"Of course."

Early in their dating relationship, Ben had told Marla about his son Bartolome – a son he knew about, but had never met. He'd shared all the details with her, and after they were married he'd mention Bartolome, now and then. But she wasn't prepared for what he'd told her the day before as soon as he arrived home from the office.

"Marla, I need to talk with you," he'd said, setting his briefcase down. "Can we have some time now without Danielle intruding?"

"No promises, but she's sleeping. What's up?"

Ben led her into their living room, and motioned for her to sit with him on the oversized sofa. It was then Marla noticed the letter-sized manila envelope in his hand.

"I've told you everything I know about Bartolome, but I didn't think it was necessary to show you these letters. Now I want you to read them."

"Bartolome? Has something happened?" she asked, with concern in her voice.

He handed her the first letter. It was from a law firm in Spain, dated in August of 2008.

Dear Sr. Benjamin Taylor:

This letter comes to you at the instruction of our client, Maria Teresa Laureano. Since it is common in our country to shorten first names, you may have known her as Maite Laureano.

Our beloved Maite passed away peacefully on 25th July of this year. Before she died, she asked us to contact you after she was gone so that you might receive her letter. It is enclosed.

We have very strict laws regarding what she is sharing with you. All we can tell you is Bartolome is with a wonderful and loving family who are deserving of this beautiful child.

If you choose to contact us, we will, of course, be polite with you. But we cannot, and will not, do anything more than what we have already done with this communication.

The letter was signed by Estela Ana Demara, who Ben told Marla was an attorney in the firm's Valencia office.

Marla handed the letter back, and Ben gave her a second one – handwritten, and dated July 2, 2008.

My Dear Benjamin,

I hope this letter finds you well and happy.

I have very little time, so please forgive my directness. We, you and I, have a son. And I am dying.

Our son's name is Bartolome. In Spanish, Bartolome is Benjamin, and I'm told he prefers Bart. He is now five years old.

I became pregnant one of our few times together. Soon after, I learned I had cancer. I was healthy enough to have Bartolome, but not to care for him. I had him for a few wonderful days at the hospital, then gave him to the finest adoption agency in all of Spain. I know because many years ago they found a home for me after my parents died.

They offered to let me meet our son's new parents, but I was too weak and heartbroken. All I know is he is with wonderful people who love and care for him as I would. And, I hope, as would you.

By the time you receive this from my lawyer, I will have gone to be with Our Lord. Please don't hate me for what I've done. For not telling you before the birth, and for not asking you about the adoption. I did what I thought best, and I've lived with the pain, and the shame. I can't change what has happened, and I pray you will find it in your heart to forgive me.

With love,

Maite

Again, after reading silently, Marla returned the letter to Ben. Then she said, "Ben, you've already told me everything in these letters.

And that you went to Spain in search of Bartolome, but the law firm wouldn't help you. You said even the private investigators you hired were of no help. So why now?"

"This arrived today," he answered, withdrawing another letter from the envelope and handing it to her.

Dear Sr. Benjamin Taylor:

I am writing to inform you there has been a development regarding Maria Teresa Laureano's son Bartolome. Please don't be alarmed. Bartolome is in excellent health and doing fine in every regard.

Please call the undersigned at the number indicated at your convenience.

Yours faithfully.

Estela Ana Demara

Her hand was moist when she handed it back, her mouth dry when she ended an awkward silence with, "I know what the letter *says*. But what does it *mean*? To you? To us?"

"Marla, I don't know what it means. I only read it an hour ago."

"What do you want me to do?"

"I want you to be on the call with me when I talk with the lawyer. I exchanged emails with her assistant, and we'll be talking tomorrow morning at nine, our time."

The conference call the next day was brief. Marla and Ben learned Bartolome was now thirteen, and his adoptive parents were cautiously considering his request to meet his father. When the parent's agreed to the lawyer's suggestion of an adults-only meeting as a first step, the lawyers contacted Ben to determine if he also had an interest.

Jo listened patiently, and attentively, for several uninterrupted minutes as Marla conveyed her feelings of anxiety and concern. Marla ended by saying Ben would be going to Spain in a few weeks.

Jo knew she had to proceed cautiously since she couldn't yet share what had occurred in her own home the previous day. Marla had no way of knowing she was talking with the woman who would soon become Bartolome's step-grandmother.

"Marla, I'm not certain what you're asking."

"I guess I'm not really asking anything. I just wanted to share it with you – as a friend. It was a surprise, of course. A big one. I've had time to think about it, and I'm happy for Ben. I truly am. But I *am* worried about how it's all going to work out."

Relieved, Jo said, "I know this is all so new to you and Ben. I'm going to encourage you to be patient, to let things play out. And I know that's much easier said than done." Thinking back on *her* last 24 hours, Jo asked, "What about The Judge. Does he know?"

"He doesn't. Ben tried to reach him last night, but couldn't find him. He's going to call him today."

Jo smiled to herself since she knew why Ben's father went missing the previous evening.

"Marla, I know you can't help worrying about what all this means. And everything is so uncertain now. But I think you'll find most things worrying you now won't happen, and you wouldn't have been able to change the things that do happen."

"I remember reading something like that in your journals. And there was more to it."

"It says it's often not what happens to you, but what you *think* happened, that's important. As is how you respond, or don't respond. Marla, I learned a long time ago not every ball that's thrown my way must be caught. Sometimes, it's better to just let some bounce away."

20

Jo's happiness about being with the most important people in her life at Thanksgiving mixed with feelings of anxiety. She knew her appearance was changing, and the last thing she wanted was sympathy, spoken or unspoken.

"Just yourselves," Marla told Jo when she called to ask what she could bring to the gathering in a few days in Bowling Green.

November 23rd arrived, and Ben met Jo and the Fleners at the entrance to an enclosed ground-level parking garage behind the Park Row building. The elevator rose to the second floor, and they all stepped into a hallway with a door in each direction. Jo remembered Marla saying one was The Judge's residence, the other a guest suite that could be used for a caregiver if one was needed in The Judge's later years – years both she and The Judge knew they wouldn't be sharing with each other. It was something they talked about openly the night they finally shared their feelings for each other.

Ben led them to the door on the left, opening it to reveal a beautifully decorated residence with a fully-stocked kitchen. Jo insisted that Charlie and Ruth be shown to the master suite, with her occupying the second of three bedrooms. A five-star hotel couldn't have been more tastefully elegant, or more welcoming.

A beautiful display of fresh cut flowers graced the dining room table, as well as three envelopes, two addressed to Jo, and one to the Fleners. Ruth began brewing a pot of coffee and, after unpacking, they all reconvened a few minutes later. Sitting at the table, Ruth opened their card, smiling as she read it before showing to Charlie, and then Jo. It was a short note of welcome, signed by Marla, Ben and The Judge. Jo opened, read and shared the ones addressed to her from Marla and Ben, and from Jennings and Lucy Mae.

It was only a few minutes past noon, but Jo excused herself to lie down for a while. She knew the rest of the day would be longer than she'd become accustomed to, and she wanted to be at her best. At her *very* best. Ben had told them his father would arrive from Frankfort later, and the plan was for everyone to gather in The Judge's suite at three, with Thanksgiving dinner to follow in the upstairs residence.

Jo fell asleep almost immediately, and it seemed as if only a few minutes had passed when she heard Ruth's gentle knock at the door at two-thirty. Jo knew the changes in her appearance were slight, but they *were* noticeable. Her hair was beginning to thin, along with the rest of her. She'd always been careful about her diet, and exercised as much as her condition over the years would allow. She'd never had a weight problem, until now, and it's the opposite of what befalls most women as they age.

Marla had assured Jo the attire was casual, and Jo made certain the items she selected had been altered by a seamstress she'd used for years. Clothes had been an indulgence she'd allowed herself as she became successful, and she learned early on you get what you pay for. With careful selection, and a flair for "mix and match," she'd been able to create a somewhat timeless wardrobe.

For most of her company's almost thirty-year existence, Jo had been its public persona, and there was no escaping the dramatically different fashion expectations separating professional women and men. She also wouldn't deny she'd compensated for those early years when all her mother could afford were clothes others had worn – either donated to Goodwill when Jo was in elementary and high school, or consigned to specialty stores when she was in college. Now, it made no sense to buy new clothes as her weight began to change. Skillful alteration would do just fine.

They knocked on the door to The Judge's residence a few minutes before three. Jo's fiancée opened the door, greeted the Fleners warmly, and kissed Jo on her cheek as she entered. Jennings and Lucy Mae, already seated in matching high-back chairs to the left of the fireplace, stood to greet them. The Eldridges had known the Fleners for years because of Jo, as had Beverly Wingate, who also rose from her chair to hug both Charlie and Ruth. A few minutes later, Marla and Ben arrived, completing the Thanksgiving guest list, and the audience for the upcoming announcement.

Jo searched the faces of Jennings, Lucy Mae and Beverly for any reaction to her appearance. Nothing. They *had* to notice the difference, but they had so much class that they hid the recognition Jo knew was there. She did so love them all.

Despite The Judge's "no big deal" assurances, Jo realized she was holding her breath in anticipation. But he was right. She watched everyone as The Judge announced their engagement, and the only surprised expressions belonged to Marla and Ben, although their response was enthusiastic and heartfelt. Everyone else reacted in an "it's about time" manner, with hugging and handshaking accompanied by expressions of happiness and best wishes. After a celebratory toast offered by Ben, they adjourned to the upstairs residence, where they were greeted by a feast prepared by Marla, Lucy Mae and Beverly.

At the end of the meal, they moved to the living room for coffee or after-dinner drinks. Jo remained standing, and when everyone was comfortably seated, said, "I must excuse myself. It's been a wonderful evening, and the dinner was one for the ages. But I'm feeling very tired, and need to call it a day. Thank you all for my most enjoyable Thanksgiving ever."

There were hugs and kisses with everyone before Jo made her exit, accompanied by Charlie and Ruth, who graciously said they were also tired. The Judge joined them, but when they reached the guest residence, Jo insisted that he return to be with the others on this special day for families and friends. He kissed and hugged her, and reluctantly departed.

Like most writers, Marla was thinking about her current project, even on a holiday. She'd asked Jo earlier if she could have some time to discuss the book. And she'd agreed with Jo that since Ruth and Charlie had known Jo so well and so intimately over the years, their thoughts could have value. They agreed to have breakfast the next morning in the guest suite. Jo slept well, and awoke refreshed and energized. She insisted on making breakfast, and was just putting everything on the table when Marla arrived at eight-thirty.

As they were eating, Marla began by saying, "I've been organizing and re-organizing, and my enthusiasm remains undiminished. If anything, it's growing, as is the size of the book."

Since Jo had encouraged Charlie and Ruth to be active participants, Ruth asked, "How big?"

"At least three-hundred pages if published in its current form. Upwards of a hundred-thousand words."

"That sounds ambitious," Charlie commented. "Jo, is that what you were anticipating?"

"Truthfully, I wasn't anticipating anything specific. I've had so little time to focus on it, and won't until after the ESOP is completed the end of next month. Marla, let's just agree for you to keep plowing ahead."

They continued to discuss content and its organization, and Jo complimented Marla on her organizational skills, her writing, and her hard work.

"Oh, Jo, I just remembered a question," Marla said. "Some time ago, you mentioned the term *glass cliff* when we talked about glass ceilings. What did you mean?"

"It's a term for when women accept high profile positions with companies in distress, thinking it may be their only ticket to a corner office. Failure is highly probable for either a male or female executive, but a woman will most likely be judged more harshly, and her career may go off a cliff."

Their book discussion, and their breakfast, had just ended when there was a knock at the door.

"Come in. It's not locked," Marla said.

Ben entered, with a very troubled look on his face.

"Jo, we need to talk. Can you join us in Dad's residence?"

"Sounds urgent," she said, rising.

"Don't worry about the dishes, or anything," Ruth said.

"And I'll stay to help. You go on," Marla added.

They hurried down to The Judge's suite. It was Black Friday, the shopping day after Thanksgiving. Jo soon learned this day would be black for another reason.

"Bad news. Actually, potentially very bad news," Ben said as Jo, Jennings and The Judge settled in around the dining room table.

"What is it, Ben?" Jo asked. Her heart was pounding.

"I was called to the office early this morning. Hadn't planned on going in, but the team working on the ESOP said they had to talk to me."

"And?" Jennings asked.

"One of the lawyers discovered a covenant in the largest line of credit at Jo's company, one vital to its operation. It's a provision that requires Jo to be functioning in an active, day-to-day CEO leadership role or the funding can be interrupted, even potentially cancelled."

A lengthy discussion ensued, but the conclusion remained unchanged. If Jo leaves the company for any reason, the funding would be in jeopardy.

"That's the problem." Jo said. "Now, what are the solutions?"

"In order to see the ESOP happen, you'll have to remain as CEO until we can secure replacement financing," Ben answered. "And we'll have to do it carefully without alerting people inside and outside the company."

"How long do you think that will take?" The Judge asked.

"I've only had an hour or so to process this," Ben answered, "but my best guess, given all the complexities, is at least two months. Maybe longer."

Jo looked away from the others to process what she'd heard. The day had dawned sunny, but very cold. Through the floor-to-ceiling windows she could see the few leaves stubbornly remaining on tree branches gently moving with the wind gusts. Soon they would be blowing around on the ground in the Town Square below, their beauty gone, their life ended.

"Just so I'm understanding correctly, all of our plans are on hold?" she asked as she turned around, hoping all three men would mistakenly believe her tears were related to financing problems.

"Unfortunately, Jo," Ben answered, handing her a napkin, "everything depends upon the perception that you're actively leading the company. Once we get the new financing, the ESOP can happen. But it will be sometime later next year, not in a few weeks as we had all planned."

A lot more had been planned than just transferring ownership and leadership of her company. There was her new life with The Judge, free of all the stress and time commitment that was now going to continue to dominate her life.

Once they had exhausted the financing discussion, Jo excused herself to finish packing for the drive back to Bardstown. The Judge said he would drive up later in the afternoon, so he wasn't with her when she got the phone message.

21

J o played the message again, and again, not wanting to believe a terrible day had just gotten worse.

As a gift to herself, and a courtesy to the others, Jo had turned off her cell phone when they arrived in Bowling Green, and didn't turn it back on until they were in the car and their journey home was well underway. Not surprisingly, there were several messages, even given the holiday. One was from her primary care physician in Lexington.

"Your tests results are back, and we need to see you as soon as possible. Can you come to our office tomorrow?"

"Tomorrow" was Saturday, a day the doctor's office was closed. If it couldn't wait until Monday, Jo thought, it had to be very bad news, and called back to confirm she'd be there at the requested time.

Charlie was driving, with Ruth beside him. Jo leaned forward from the backseat, touched his right shoulder, and asked if she could impose upon him to drive her to an appointment in the morning. He wasn't scheduled to work, but without asking what, where or why, he answered, "Of course."

The Judge arrived at Jo's home a few hours after her and, when he heard the news, insisted on accompanying her the next morning. They bundled up against the cold, and went for a long walk in a nearby park. They watched old movies on television. They talked about many things, but not about what was foremost on their minds. They had an early dinner and went to bed around ten, but both were still awake well after midnight. When Marla told Jo recently that she had difficulty dealing with uncertainty, Jo's answer had been that most people do. Now she was facing uncertainty of her own, with no expectation hers would end well the next day.

Meetings with her doctor seldom exceeded thirty minutes. This one lasted for over an hour, with both The Judge and Charlie at her side. The drive back to her house took less than twenty minutes, and all three rode in almost complete silence.

Ruth was waiting for them, and had thoughtfully prepared an early lunch. They gathered around the food-laden table, but it served only as a place to talk. All their appetites had evaporated with the news. The test results revealed Jo was experiencing an advanced stage of kidney failure, a known complication for many suffering with sickle-cell anemia.

Charlie had asked if he could share the prognosis with Ruth, and Jo nodded. With aggressive treatment, and frequent hospitalization, Jo might live another two or three years. Without it, the upcoming Christmas would be her last. When Ruth asked if a kidney transplant was possible, Jo knew she wasn't up for sharing the information they deserved. She said she needed to lie down for a while, and The Judge walked her upstairs to her bedroom. *Their* bedroom.

At the doorway, Jo collapsed into his arms, crying. Before she knew what was happening, he picked her up and carried her into the room, gently laying her on the bed. As he tucked the comforter around her, her tears turned to laughter.

Sitting on the edge of the bed, he waited for her to explain.

"I just realized that something I dreamed about as a teenager just happened."

"And that would be?"

"To be carried over a threshold by my husband."

"About-to-be husband," clarified a now-smiling Judge. "I hope it's not me that made you laugh."

"No. Not at all. What got me laughing, maybe to keep from crying, was the thought that I had to be dying to have that dream fulfilled. Macabre, I know, but I couldn't control myself."

"Jo, *controlling* yourself should no longer be a concern. You're entitled to behave any way you want. We both are, and to hell with what anyone else thinks."

"Judge, please go back down and tell Ruth and Charlie everything. We can't just leave things where they are. They're as close to me, to us, as family, and they should know."

It was mid-afternoon when she awoke, and the first thing she saw was *her* Judge, sitting in a chair next to the bed. Holding her hand, he looked at her with a mix of love and concern.

"Hungry?" he asked.

"Only for you. And for time. How did it go with Ruth and Charlie?"

The Judge shared in detail the conversation they'd had while she was sleeping. It began with Charlie asking why the doctors hadn't talked about possible cures, like a transplant.

"Charlie said he and Ruth had talked about it while I was upstairs," The Judge said, "and they both wanted to be considered as possible donors."

"What did you tell them?"

"Thanked them for their thoughtfulness, and that I would share their offer with you. And then I told them why it wasn't possible."

Charlie and Ruth had known for years that Jo had SCA because one or both of them was with her at most of her doctor appointments, lab visits, and occasional hospitalizations. She was diagnosed in elementary school, so while her mind was anxious for her to participate in competitive athletics, her body wasn't able. It was then she learned her mother also had the disease, as did her father. Jo learned in college the things about SCA that resulted in the decision she and Barrey made to not have children.

"I told them your mother suffered kidney failure when she was about the age you are now, and that you were tested as a potential donor. I told them other complications of the disease made the transplant unfeasible, and your mother passed away."

The re-telling of what she'd lived with for so many years caused Jo to start crying again, interrupting The Judge's recounting of his conversation. When she regained her composure, she asked, "And you told them about Agnes?"

"I did."

◆ ◆ ◆

Agnes Beale was a single mother of four with a rare auto-immune disorder who was going to die without a kidney transplant. Jo's donor information, completed when she envisioned her mother as the recipient, was still on file in a database. Years after her mother died, Jo was contacted because she was as close to a perfect donor match for Agnes as possible. Jo had a decision to make, and not an easy one.

She'd known for many years that the only possible, and very uncertain, cure for SCA was a bone marrow transplant once the illness advanced to a certain stage. And her doctors told her the two procedures – transplant and kidney donation – for her would be mutually exclusive. She couldn't be a kidney donor for Agnes, and then later receive a bone marrow transplant, or be the *recipient* of a kidney donation in the event her remaining kidney failed.

She could choose to save a life by being a donor, or *possibly* extend her own with an operation in the future. No one, she thought, should have to make such a choice. And given Agnes' precarious condition, she only had a few days to decide. Although she chose not to burden anyone else with her deliberation, that wasn't entirely true. She prayed.

Jo made the decision to be a donor without knowing the identity of the recipient. Two days later, after being prepped for surgery, both patients met for the first time, lying on gurneys outside the operating room. Until that moment, their names hadn't been disclosed to the other. They both began crying because they realized they knew each other! Agnes was a long-term employee of Jo's company, and they occasionally had lunch together in the cafeteria.

The operation was a complete success, with Agnes and Jo sharing the same recovery room. When both were strong enough for the conversation, and were alone, Jo pleaded with her not to disclose her as the donor.

"Why not? Agnes had asked. "You saved my life! I want everyone to know what a wonderful thing you did."

But Jo was insistent, and Agnes agreed not to say anything so that other employees wouldn't treat either of them differently. But she assured Jo that her gratitude would be in her eyes whenever they were together.

To Jo's complete surprise, the media got ahold of the story because of Agnes being a single mother and the potential impact on her children if she hadn't survived. Had she died without the transplant, the children would have been separated into multiple foster homes. Jo dispatched one of her attorneys to the hospital to reinforce, in no uncertain terms, her insistence on remaining anonymous, and the severe legal consequences for the hospital if that anonymity was ever compromised. It never was.

◆ ◆ ◆

The Judge's voice brought her back to the present.

"Jo, I know all this has been a terrible shock for you today. When you're ready to tell others, just let me know, and I'll make the arrangements."

"I've kept so much of my illness from you and Jennings. Now I need to know what both of you think of the two options the doctors *did* give us today. Would you see if Jennings can meet with us here tomorrow?"

22

Jo had fixed a light breakfast of fruit and toast, The Judge's favorite, and they were sitting at the small table in a nook just off the kitchen. Jennings and Lucy Mae were expected within the hour.

"Jo, the choice is yours, and I'll love and support you either way you decide."

"I know you will. But what I really want to know now, before Jennings gets here, is what *you* think."

"I think the choices are terrible, and it comes down to two things – time, and the suffering you'll have to endure." Jo didn't reply, forcing him to continue. Unless she heard something from either her husband or Jennings that she hadn't thought of, her decision had been made.

"Selfishly, I want as much time with you as possible. But that choice means much of it will be spent in treatment, and I'm guessing a lot of time in hospitals and doctor's offices. From what I understand, those treatments can be painful, with awful side effects."

"And it would mean I'd have to leave the company right away," Jo added, "and abandon the ESOP. And my foundation."

"That's the business side, of course, and others can labor over those consequences. I'm only focused on you. And the two to three years they told us it might mean for you. For us."

"I know, and I love you for it. But I also heard them say there were no promises about the time, only estimates. What about the other?"

"Jo, *that* becomes a business decision. You can't have both. If you stay with the company, you can't undergo the treatments." And they both had heard the doctors say the "business choice" meant she wouldn't live out the coming year.

"Judge, before Jennings and Lucy Mae get here, there's something I have to tell you. And I want you to take your time before answering. Okay?"

"Not knowing what you're going to say," he answered, "it's hard to know if I'll need time."

"Promise me."

"Okay, I promise."

"I want you to re-think your marriage proposal."

He started to say something, but she held up her hand as a plea to let her finish.

"You didn't sign on for this. You knew I had SCA, but neither of us knew what that really meant. Now we know, and the consequences either way we decide. I've loved you, in different ways, at different times, all my life. And I can say, with all the love I have for you in my heart at this moment, I'll understand if you don't want to become a widower again. And so soon."

"Jo, there is no way on God's earth I want another day to go by without being married to you. Time was never a certainty for us. Because of your illness, and my age, which by the way is something you never once mentioned."

Jo started to speak, but The Judge was quicker. "Now, if you'll please excuse me," he said, "there's something I need to do before our guests arrive."

Curious when she heard the front door open and close, Jo looked out the living room window and saw him pull his cell phone from the pocket of his sports coat and dial a number. She wasn't able to hear anything, but could tell he made two calls, neither of which lasted more than a couple of minutes. As he was returning the phone to his pocket, Richard approached her from behind and announced that their guests had just passed through the entrance gate.

Jo watched as the two life-long friends embraced after Jennings exited the driver's side of his modest Chrysler. And it appeared to be a contest to see which one could get to the passenger side to open the door for Lucy Mae. The Judge won.

Once they were all settled in the living room, Jo wanted to get right to it.

"Thank you so much for coming on such short notice. And without knowing the reason."

"Don't need a reason, my dear," Lucy Mae said. "Seeing you, and getting Jennings out of town for a beautiful winter drive, are reason enough."

"Well, there *is* a reason. And not a pleasant one. Judge, I'd prefer if you be the one to…"

The Judge picked up on her incomplete sentence and explained, briefly and eloquently, what they'd learned the previous day. When he finished, Lucy Mae was crying softly, and Jennings, although maintaining a stoic countenance, had tears brimming his brilliant blue eyes.

"Jo and Judge," Jennings began, his voice slightly cracking, "I don't know what to say. Except that we love both of you so much, and will do anything we can to help."

"We know that," Jo said, "and we invited you today to ask you to help us think through what to do. But I've made my decision."

The Judge looked surprised, but said nothing. Everyone remained quiet, waiting to hear.

"I've decided to remain with the company. To not go through with the treatments."

They all remained silent, waiting for her to continue.

"I've lived with this disease almost all my life. I saw how it took my mother from me, and I don't want that experience. I know what the treatments involve. And I'd rather have a couple of months of anything approaching a normal life than a year or two in a hospital bed. I'm not going to do that to myself, and I'm not going to put Judge through it."

It was apparent they wanted to hear her out without interrupting. In their position, she'd do the same, so she decided to hasten through the rest of it. "Apart from the impact on Judge and me, and other great friends like you, going this way means I can finish the ESOP. Completing that means everything I want for my foundation after I'm gone will also happen. So, that's it. That's my decision."

It appeared each one was about to speak at the same time, so to head off a protracted "yes, but" discussion questioning her painful decision, she added, "Oh, one other thing. This morning I offered Judge a get-out-of-jail-free card, but he stubbornly insists on going through with marrying me."

"Then what are we waiting for? Let's have a wedding," Lucy Mae said, slapping her knee.

"Today?" Jennings asked. "Won't it take some doing, some preparation? Ours was so long ago I don't remember."

"That's because my mother and I did everything. All you said you were going to do is show up, look presentable and say 'I do.' And aren't you glad you did?"

"Lucy Mae," Jennings said, smiling, "I'm sure The Judge and Jo are as captivated as I am by your walk down *our* memory lane, but let's get back to them."

"It's all taken care of. We'll leave in about an hour," The Judge said.

"Where are we going?" Jo asked.

"Frankfort. To get married. A few minutes before Jennings and Lucy Mae arrived, I called Hewitt and asked him to make the necessary arrangements. He'll be waiting at the court."

Hewitt Emerson Chandler was another Kentucky Supreme Court Justice, and The Judge's closest friend and colleague on the bench. Understanding she was about to become Mrs. Benjamin Taylor, Sr., Jo assumed Hewitt was The Judge's first phone call, Ben the second.

"What about Ben and Marla?" Jo asked.

"I talked with Ben a little while ago," The Judge replied. "He said the doctors think Danielle will recover fully, but she hasn't been cleared to travel. Marla is adamant that Ben be with us, so he'll meet us there – if he doesn't get arrested for speeding."

"Oh, he will, will he? So, let me see if I have this straight," Jo said, trying to act indignant, but not fooling anyone. "As we speak, your son is already driving – speeding – to *my* wedding. A wedding I'm just this minute finding out about. And I'm the bride."

"Uh, huh," the groom answered. "Is an hour enough time for you to get ready?"

Within an hour, Charlie and Ruth arrived. Jennings and Lucy Mae rode with them, and Jo and The Judge rode in the Town Car with Richard at the wheel. At almost precisely noon, on November 26, 2016, standing in the Chief Justice's chambers in Frankfort, they were married.

Ben made it in time, and stood with his father. Lucy Mae was Matron of Honor, and for the first time ever, Jennings allowed himself to be considered a surrogate father to Jo. Ruth and Charlie had worked their magic, and there was a bouquet of Jo's favorite flowers already in Justice Chandler's office by the time they arrived.

They celebrated over lunch at a private club where both Jennings and The Judge were members. Jo had been there many times over the years, in particular when Jennings' business brought him to Frankfort and an opportunity presented itself for the three of them to be together.

Their celebration concluded at about two in the afternoon. Ben congratulated the newlyweds, telling Jo the kiss was from Marla and

Danielle. He embraced his father, and whispered in his ear, "Dad, I'm so very happy for you. And for Jo."

After Ben said good-bye to the others and departed for the drive home, The Judge invited Jennings and Lucy Mae to spend the night at the Bardstown residence.

"Not a chance," was Jennings' immediate response.

"Why?" The Judge asked.

"Two reasons." Jennings paused for dramatic effect and waited to be asked.

"Okay, what are the two reasons why you won't stay with Mrs. Taylor and me tonight?"

"First, we didn't come prepared for an overnight. You know, clothes and things."

Again, the dramatic pause.

"And?" The Judge asked.

"And what?"

"The second reason. Or can't you remember back that far?" The Judge playfully bantered. "To what you said thirty seconds ago?"

"It's your wedding night, old boy. She's too much of a lady to say anything, but I doubt Jo would welcome our presence. And I know *my* bride would agree."

Slapping his arm, Lucy Mae said, "Jennings, behave yourself! But we really should get going to retrieve our car so we can get home before dark. My husband, master of the universe that he is, shouldn't be driving after dark. Neither of us should."

As they were saying their good-byes an hour later back in Bardstown, The Judge asked if Jo was up for a day trip down to Bowling Green the next day to tell Ben and Marla what they'd already shared with others about her medical condition. Before she could answer in the affirmative, Jennings couldn't resist a parting shot.

"Might want to re-think that. See if you're up to it. You know, the morning after the night before. You're not as young as you were first time around, Judge. Being a brand new husband, with a much younger wife. Just a suggestion."

Jennings was rewarded with the laughter he sought. But Jo's new husband held his own.

"Thank you for your advice, which you so readily offered in mixed company. But as you drive home, be thinking of the words of that Toby Keith song we both like."

"Help me, Judge, what words?"

"I'm not as good as I once was, but I'm as good once as I ever was."

"I bow to you, my friend," Jennings replied. Then the two men embraced.

"See what you've gotten yourself into?" Lucy asked. "Two little boys wanting the whole world to perceive them as grown-up, responsible men. Now you know the truth."

"Lucy Mae, I've known the truth about these two all my life. Boys or men, I don't care. All I care about is that they love me, and will as long as I live."

Jo didn't mean to say that in the way she was now afraid it would be interpreted. As an invitation to feel sorry for her.

"Oh, please, I didn't mean…"

"We know," The Judge said, rescuing her as he placed his right arm around her waist.

They waved to the departing car, said good-bye to Ruth and Charlie, and walked back toward the house.

"Penny for your thoughts," Jo said, as a strong arm pulled her closer.

"They're worth more than that. Much more."

"Dollar?"

"Done," The Judge replied. "It was something Jennings said."

23

Jo had welcomed The Judge's suggestion of a modest local diner for their evening meal. It had been a long, emotional and tiring day for her, but it had been years since she could recall seeing The Judge as invigorated as he appeared. All day long. She then remembered something, and reached into her purse, retrieved a dollar bill, and slid it across the table.

"What's that for?" The Judge asked.

"Your thoughts. Bought and paid for at the price we negotiated. Remember?"

"I do."

"And?" Jo asked. "You said it was something Jennings had said."

"Well, at that very moment on the porch, when you offered a penny for my thoughts, I was thinking it was the night before the morning after. Just as he said."

Happily for Jo, *invigorated* continued well after they returned home. Something she mentioned, but only *after,* as they lay together.

"Jo, yesterday when we left the doctor's office, I felt as if it were the end of the world. But today, my world began all over again. I know what's ahead of us, and it breaks my heart knowing what could have been, if only I'd acted years and years ago. I'm an old man in love with a beautiful younger woman who just became my wife. Why wouldn't I be acting this way?"

"And you've made me so very happy, Judge. But please don't spend time thinking of what might have been. Neither of us acted on our feelings. And the trite expression I used to hate – *better late than never* – really does apply to us. All I ask now is that you embrace the thinking of that great American philosopher, Leonardo DiCaprio."

"The actor?"

"Yep."

"It's late," The Judge said. "We're both tired. May I ask that we dispense with the back and forth that will ultimately result in you telling me Leonardo's words of wisdom?"

"Oh, all right. It was the dinner scene from the movie *Titanic*. When he said his life was guided by one simple principal – to make each day count."

"Well said. Jo, I promise to follow the teachings of Leonardo, and I can see what led to your suggestion. The words are inspiring, but so was your vision of a younger-older manifestation of your ideal male."

Jo raised herself up on her right elbow, and looked lovingly in the dim light at the man beside her. Then she burst out laughing.

"Overreaching?" he asked, defensively.

"*No man*, including Leonardo, could measure up to you in my eyes. This is just a side of you I've never seen before. Maybe no one else has either."

"Well, I have certain proprieties to maintain."

"No, you *don't*. Not any longer. Your retirement means you can just be yourself. *This* self. To me, and others. But especially me."

Day Two as Mrs. Benjamin Taylor Sr. was again sunny, but warmer than Day One by at least fifteen degrees. Jo was becoming increasingly sensitive to the cold, so that was a welcomed change. After breakfast, Charlie drove them to Bowling Green to meet with Marla and Ben.

When Ben opened the door, they could smell the aroma of cinnamon rolls Marla had made just for the occasion. Ben said "Hi, Mom" before hugging her and kissing her on the cheek.

"Oh, I don't *think* so," Jo answered, smiling as broadly as he was. "I was thinking more along the lines of Mrs. Judge. Or perhaps just Jo. Your choice."

"Jo, it is. Here, let me take your coat," Ben said as he turned to shake his father's hand. "Congratulations, Dad. I'm so happy for you."

"Oh, I'm so happy for both of you," Marla said enthusiastically, entering the room and heading to hug and kiss their guests.

After this light-hearted start to the visit, the atmosphere grew somber as they sat in the living room. Even the inviting cinnamon smells couldn't stir any of their appetites after The Judge shared the news about Jo's failing health. Marla reacted with tears, and a few questions. Ben attempted the manly-man demeanor, but his heart was breaking for Jo, and for his father. The Judge had supported Ben when he dealt with the tragic death of two of his wives, and now their roles would be reversed.

"I know this is a lot for you to take in all at once," Jo said. "We appreciate your offers to help, and we'll certainly be counting on you in the future. But for now, it's enough to know you're thinking of us, and will be there when we need you. And need you we will."

"Jo, I want to offer all this up in prayer." With heads bowed, and hands held, Marla asked for a healing presence in Jo's life and strength for all of them.

At Jo's request, they turned down the invitation to stay for lunch, and headed for home. Emotionally and physically drained by all that had occurred over the past thirty-six hours, she had reached her endurance limit. And the next day began a new work week.

As Jo watched the passing scenery on the drive home, her thoughts were on business. Could she really pull this off? Could she keep up the necessary CEO appearances as her physical appearance noticeably declined? She knew she'd give it her best on all fronts, given what was at stake for so many people depending upon her, but she also knew there were now limitations even she couldn't overcome.

When she reached over and took The Judge's hand in hers, he said, "You were someplace else there for a while, so I didn't disturb you."

"I was just thinking, worrying actually, about all I have to do now that I've made my decision."

"What can I do?" he asked.

"Be Leonardo. And remind me to do the same if I'm not."

Charlie was driving, so they sat together in the back seat. The car felt comfortably warm, and its gentle swaying, and the road noise, combined to take her away into a restful sleep as she nestled into The Judge's embrace. She was awakened when the car's motion stopped. When she sat up, she realized they were in her circular driveway.

"What's the matter?" The Judge asked when Jo stopped short of entering the house.

She pointed to the bottom of the open doorway as she mouthed "threshold." Jo's weakened condition enabled The Judge to effortlessly sweep her up into his arms.

As they passed into the foyer, she shifted her weight, signaling a desire to be returned to a standing position. As soon as she was, she kissed him, and said, "That's twice you've carried me over a threshold. My dreams coming true are now repeating."

They settled in the living room, warmed by the fire and the glow of the Christmas tree. Nestled in his arms on the sofa, Jo said, "Judge, I hate it that we'll be apart during the day. Would you consider coming with me to the office?

"I want to be with you as much as possible, but won't I be a distraction from your work? And won't it look odd to your employees to have me just hanging around?"

"I have an idea. And if you agree, you'll be as busy as me. It's something that's now extremely important to me, and I need your help. Actually, *we* need your help."

"*We?*"

When she explained, he agreed since it *would* enable them to be together more. But he expressed doubt about his ability to contribute.

"Judge, the only one who may be surprised by your contribution will be you. We have complete confidence in you, and I can't wait to make the call in the morning."

24

Their book had become a casualty of Jo's rapidly declining health, but Marla continued to read the journals and play the recordings of their conversations. She was sitting in her home office, listening to a recording and reminiscing about happier times just a few months earlier when she'd spent hours there almost every day, working on the project.

Jo: "I was ten when I knew I wanted to be successful in business, and began my journals."

Marla: "That young? What got you started?"

Jo: "It began when Mother took me with her to Mr. Eldridge's country club. She worked in the kitchen, and as a waitress. The members were always nice to me. Most of them, anyway. And they didn't seem to mind me being around. I couldn't help hearing them talk, and when something was said that made an impact on me, I slipped away and wrote it down in a little notebook I kept in my book bag."

Marla: "What did these men say that made a girl of ten want to write it down?"

Jo: "Many things. I didn't fully understand everything I wrote down right away, but I knew they needed money to be able to afford a country club. I learned some of them had family money, but mostly they were successful businessmen. So anything they said about their successes, their failures or their challenges interested me."

Marla: "Was it only business things?"

Jo: "Oh, no. I learned a lot about tolerance and intolerance as I listened to them discussing current events. They talked about the violence and riots that marred the country in the sixties, but Bowling Green was virtually untouched by racial tension. They also talked about the anti-Vietnam War movement, and other things happening in the late 1960s and early 1970s."

Marla: "Didn't you, or your mother, think it was unusual that these white men were so accepting of having you, a little black girl, in such close proximity to them during their discussions?"

Jo: "I didn't think about it at the time. But I'm sure it was a combination of things. I was certainly non-threatening. And respectful, never saying anything unless I was spoken to. I often helped Mother as a server, so there was a reason for me to be in the dining room. I have no way of knowing now, but they may have been respectful of what was most likely understood to be a special relationship between Mother and Jennings' family. It was a very small town, after all."

Marla: "How did you know at such a young age you wanted to be a businesswoman? That was quite ambitious, and forward-thinking."

Jo: "For a girl?"

Marla: "I'm sorry, Jo. I didn't mean to offend you. Really I didn't. I was only speaking about age."

Jo: "No offense taken. The short answer is I wanted things for Mother and me that would only be possible with money. Truthfully, I wanted what they had."

Marla: "When you were listening to these men, writing things down, aspiring to emulate them..."

Jo: "And?"

Marla: "Well, I was wondering if, even at that tender age, you were processing the very significant difference between their *current* circumstances and your *future* circumstances as a woman of color."

Jo: "It was a long time ago, but I honestly don't think so. In my child's mind, I probably thought what I was hearing were both gender and color neutral. Like we discussed with my journal entries. Oh, I knew the difference between being a black girl and a white girl in the 1960s in Kentucky. But I had my dreams, and making them come true, for Mother and me, became my focus."

Marla: "Jo, we've talked so much about success. What do you think of failure?"

Jo: It happens, of course. A lot. I never thought it was a sin to try and fail. Over and over and over again. I believe the sin is in never *trying* to succeed."

Marla: "Speaking of sin, do you have a favorite scripture that's held meaning for you? I'm thinking in terms of your business life."

Jo: "That's easy. Mark 9:23. It says all things are possible to those who believe."

Marla: "Why am I not surprised?"

Marla finished that side of the tape, and was about to play another when she heard the door open, signaling Ben was home from Spain.

After arduous Madrid-to-Dallas-to-Nashville flights, including a weather delay leaving Texas, he had secured an Uber driver to get him from the Nashville airport to Bowling Green.

They kissed and hugged for a long time, words not necessary to express how happy they both were that Ben was home. He told Marla his body clock was struggling with the two seven-hour time changes in only five days. He said he was exhausted but not sleepy.

"I need a long hot shower. That should help," Ben said, as they walked toward the kitchen. "Have you already eaten?"

"A little bit. How about I order a pizza? It can be here by the time you're back among the living, and you can tell me all about your trip."

Forty-five minutes later, over a savory meal of three-cheese pizza, salad and iced tea at the kitchen table, Ben began his debriefing. They had known before he departed that he would be meeting first with the attorneys, then the parents. He'd been given no assurance he would actually meet his son.

In the weeks before he left Bowling Green, Ben had provided the Spanish lawyers detailed written answers to dozens of questions designed to reveal as much about him as possible – personally and professionally. He complied with the request to include a copy of his passport in the courier package he sent two weeks before the scheduled meeting in Madrid. And he had submitted to DNA testing.

"The lawyers were cordial, but cautious, when we first met," Ben told Marla, "until I showed them my passport with the stamped entry from Spanish immigration when I arrived the day before."

"They just want to be certain you were you – the handsome man in the passport photo," Marla said, trying to put both of them at ease ahead of the coming conversation.

"And that's all it took. They immediately told me my DNA sample had confirmed a match with Bartolome. So there was no question – he is my son."

"Then what happened?"

"They asked me to make myself comfortable – we were in a conference room – and told me Bartolome's parents would arrive within the hour. Marla, I have to tell you, it was the longest forty-five minutes of my life. But it was worth it. They were absolutely wonderful people. If I ever had to choose adoptive parents for a child, they would be at the top of the list."

Ben then picked up his cell phone, and began showing Marla pictures taken at the lawyer's office of Ben and Bartolome's parents. And he had family photos they had forwarded to him.

"I know DNA testing is an almost exact science," Marla said, "but it wasn't necessary. Ben, your son looks exactly like you."

"He does, doesn't he?" Ben answered, proudly.

As Marla continued to look at the pictures, one in particular caught her attention. It showed a handsome boy of thirteen and the only parents he'd ever known. Everyone looked so happy, and she couldn't help wondering what all three would think about the arrival of Ben, and ultimately The Judge, Danielle and her, into their world. And now Jo, of course.

They finished their meal, agreeing to leave the cleaning up for later as they moved to the living room. Ben sat on one end of the sofa, anticipating Marla would join him, but she stood looking out one of the windows. "When you called from Madrid, you said you didn't get to meet with Bartolome."

"I didn't, and those were the ground rules. He doesn't even know at this point that they've actually found me. Parents this trip. Bartolome the next trip. Once the parents approved of me, and they said they did, they agreed to tell him and arrange for us to meet."

"When? And where?"

"I told them I wanted to talk with you before proceeding any further, and they understood."

"*They* may have understood, Ben, but I don't. He's your son, and I'm totally supportive of whatever you want to do to have him a part of your life. Our life. What do we need to discuss?"

"This has not exactly been an uneventful past couple of months for us. I didn't want to put another burden on everyone without talking with you."

"I appreciate the gesture, and the thinking behind it, but there's no way Bartolome could possibly be a burden." Marla said the words to reassure her husband, but had no way of knowing if they would prove to be true. "What do *you* want to do?"

Ben told her the parents were considering his request to bring Bartolome to Kentucky later in the year for a brief visit.

"That would be fine. But what was discussed about the future?" Marla asked.

"I asked if they would consider letting Bartolome spend some of his school breaks with us, and I was happy with their answer. They said they would let Bartolome decide."

Marla's mind was spinning, processing all the variables. They had come through a major health scare with their daughter, and Jo had just received a dire prognosis. Jo's company was in crisis, ending the book project Marla had been so looking forward to. Ben would soon be embarking on a new professional career, and Marla had decided returning to hers wasn't possible because of Danielle. And into this upheaval was coming the teenage son from her husband's affair with a woman long before Ben had entered her life.

"And if they agree to the summer visits, I'm hopeful I can persuade Bartolome, with his parent's approval, to consider attending Western," Ben added. "Just like his father, and grandfather."

"Don't forget about me, Jennings, Lucy Mae and Jo. We could form our own alumni chapter," Marla said, unable to hide the anxiety building up inside her.

"I'm sorry, Marla, have I upset you with all this? That's why I wanted us to talk before any decisions are made, and those decisions will be yours and mine, not mine."

"Ben, I know you're still wired from your trip, but I need to tend to Danielle. And wouldn't your father appreciate a call tonight with the same update you gave me?"

Ben departed to call his father, leaving Marla alone with her thoughts. She consoled herself with the knowledge Christmas was just a week away, and everyone would be together again. Ample opportunity for her to talk with Jo, and hopefully Ruth, before committing to anything regarding Bartolome. But once again, illness conspired against her.

25

During the last week of a distressing 2016, Jo and Marla spoke by phone. Both were at home.

"It was a United Nations Christmas," Jo said. "A first for us, and absolutely delightful"

"Sounds intriguing. I'd love to hear all about it."

"I didn't know what to expect when The Judge told me 'I've got it covered' after we learned so many of you were down with the flu, and Christmas in Bowling Green wasn't going to happen."

"And? Please don't keep me in suspense."

"So much happened, but I'll do my best to condense it. He arranged for our favorite restaurant to cater dinner but to prepare it in our kitchen. The chef and the server were university graduate students from overseas who didn't go home for the holidays."

"That's wonderful! Were you surprised?" Marla asked.

"Totally. And that's not all. The Judge invited four international students from the university's school of music to play for us. String instruments and my piano. All six students ate dinner with us, then joined us for Christmas Eve services at church. Afterwards, we opened presents."

"Presents?"

"Ruth and Charlie did the shopping at The Judge's request, so we had carefully selected gifts for each of our guests. They spent the night, and we all had breakfast Christmas morning before they left."

"I'm glad I didn't know, or I'd have been tempted to crawl out of my sick bed and join you."

"How *is* everyone?" Jo asked. When Marla assured her they were all recovered, they discussed a possible visit by the Versailles Taylors to the Bowling Green Taylors, but nothing was confirmed pending talking with their husbands.

The weeks immediately after the holidays are often a letdown for many people, but Jo had always thrown herself into a new year, implementing the strategies agreed upon during the preceding months of budget and business planning. But she hadn't planned on still being CEO in 2017. In fact, she resented her need to keep up a professional pretense while suffering a decline in health that was becoming increasingly difficult to disguise. And it pained her to know her employees were aware "old Jo" had not returned after the holidays. She isolated herself when she was in the office, and hoped her many absences were assumed to be business-related. When she *was* in the office, she spent many hours each day working with The Judge on their secret initiative.

The day after the January 20, 2017 presidential inauguration, they treated themselves to pie and coffee at their favorite diner, sitting on the red vinyl seats in what was becoming "their booth" because of the frequency of their evening visits.

"Penny," The Judge said.

"For my thoughts? I thought the going price was a dollar."

"Okay, a dollar." After he placed one in her outstretched hand, he said, "Jo, we've seldom talked politics, and I was wondering if you ever gave any thought to running for office?"

"Never. I was approached from time to time, emissaries I assumed had been dispatched from Jennings, and perhaps you. Was I wrong?"

"No. We thought it would be wonderful if Mary Josephine Gilpin's name would be added to Martha Layne Collins. Two women governors of Kentucky instead of just the one."

"Your kindness in thinking about me in that way was appreciated, but your confidence in my capabilities was misplaced. And it's something I never had an interest in." After pausing for a couple of seconds, she added, "That was a rather brief thought, so you still have credit remaining from your dollar. Anything else you've wondered about, but never asked?"

The Judge's hesitation was unmistakable.

"Go on. Ask," she encouraged. "Anything."

"Well, I've often wondered, as I'm sure Jennings has, if you ever considered adopting?" When she didn't immediately answer, he feared he'd sailed into choppy waters and was about to change course when she answered.

"I thought about it many times, but it wasn't something I could do. Because of my work, I would have had to go the celebrity route, adopting and then placing the child or children in the care of nannies and others. I always wanted children, and knew I would give them a very nice house to grow up in, but not a *home*. Not a home like my mother gave me."

"But it's such a beautiful home. And I think you underestimated your involvement."

"Judge, you know more about me than anyone. But no one could know everything in my heart. I am who I am because my mother's daily influence shaped me. I grew up in a home without a father, and I wouldn't do that to another child. And now….now it's too late."

Her eyes began to well up, but she didn't cry. She gave no indication of wanting to leave, so The Judge changed the subject back to politics and current events of the day.

"I think it's a great thing," Jo said, in answer to his question about what she thought of The Women's March in Washington, D.C., and in cities around the country – and around the world. "But I'm concerned. Very concerned."

"What concerns you?"

"That it's a protest," she answered, stirring the coffee she could now only enjoy in tiny sips, "and over before any good can come from it. What's needed is a movement, like the ones against the Vietnam War, or *for* civil rights."

"What keeps today's protest from becoming a movement?"

"Leadership. A movement needs a leader. For this one, it has to be a woman. A woman of substance. All of us are flawed, but she needs to be as above reproach as possible in this day of incessant twenty four-hour news cycles, most of which is bad, and often not even true."

"Where will this leader come from?" he asked.

"I don't have a clue. But while we're waiting for her, I hope women around the country will get involved in the political process. At all levels, either as candidates, or in support of women candidates. And in support of men who support women. Those men are out there. Women just need to invest the time to find them. I found mine. Actually, two. Three including Barrey."

They paid their bill, and slowly walked hand-in-hand into the parking lot. Before they reached the waiting car, she squeezed his hand as a signal to stop. Turning to look at him, she said, "Judge, I've been pretending."

"Pretending? About what?"

"Things I wanted you to think I was interested in, like movies on television, and what's going on around us."

"I'm sorry, Jo. You've lost me. I don't understand."

She did cry this time, saying, "I'm losing my eyesight.'

The Judge knew almost as much about SCA, and its complications, as any patient with the disease. Jo had learned years ago he'd begun reading up on it as soon as she was diagnosed as a child. So she didn't have to tell him what this meant now.

"When did it start?"

"Several weeks ago. It cleared up, and I thought maybe I was just tired from all that's happened. But that didn't last, and kept getting worse, so I know now it's really happening. I made an appointment for tomorrow afternoon. It's the earliest they could get me in. Go with me?"

"Of course! What time?"

"Two o'clock. Oh, and I meant to tell you. Jennings called and said he needed to meet with us tomorrow morning. About the refinancing."

"Jennings? Not Ben?"

"Must be good news for Jennings to be coming," she answered. "I hope so. I don't think I can take any more disappointments."

Jennings arrived at ten the next morning, and they convened in the living room. Despite the relaxed atmosphere, and a fire burning in the fireplace, both men were in coats and ties. It reminded Jo of so many black and white movies she'd seen from the forties and fifties. The Judge and Jennings each had a cup of coffee, Jo was sipping from a cold glass of water. Once a great consumer of coffee, she'd almost completely lost the taste for it, and her body now had difficulty with the caffeine.

"Are you the bearer of glad tidings this morning?" she asked.

"I think so. Hope so. There's been a major development, one I thought important enough for us to talk through in person. We have a tentative commitment for the financing."

"That's wonderful news, Jennings," The Judge said. "Congratulations!"

Jo reached over and placed her hand on top of her husband's, and asked Jennings why the commitment was *tentative*.

"Something we should have anticipated, but didn't. And I'll accept the blame for us not getting out ahead of it earlier."

"Ahead of what?" The Judge asked.

"The funding is conditioned upon a satisfactory presentation regarding the company's strategy, both for the coming year and a three and five-year future look."

"That shouldn't be a problem, should it? I mean, the company has been so successful."

"Judge," Jo said, now taking his hand in hers, "I think I know why Jennings is concerned. It's me, isn't it?"

The Judge turned from looking at her to looking at his friend.

"Is what Jo said true," The Judge asked, "that she's the reason the bank's commitment isn't firm?"

"Unfortunately, it is. In today's market, there isn't much opportunity for Jo's company to reduce its cost of capital by changing lenders. The interest rates are virtually identical one source to another. So the analysts underwriting the loan's potential risk are curious, maybe even suspicious. They're insisting on a full-blown boardroom presentation from the CEO."

"I've made countless of these over the years," Jo said, "so I know what's involved in the preparation. And what's at stake if the presentation isn't almost flawless."

"And you'll do wonderfully this time," The Judge said, "and the glad tidings mentioned earlier are that it'll be the last one you'll ever have to do."

Over his career, Jennings had perfected a poker face to prevent what's going on in his mind to be seen on his face. But it failed him this morning. Jo knew him so well she could tell they were thinking the same thing – that they didn't share The Judge's confidence or his enthusiasm. Jennings tilted is head slightly as a signal for her to be the one to speak.

"Judge, this is something I simply cannot do."

"Why?" he asked, obviously surprised.

"I don't have it in me. I've never been one to shy away from a challenge. But I don't have the stamina, or the ability to concentrate and think clearly, to go through the hours and hours of preparation." In an effort to lighten what was becoming the worst moment in her professional life, she added, "And to put it in terms you both can easily understand, I'm not as good once as I ever was."

"If that's the case," The Judge said, "can't your executives do all the work? Or at least most of it?"

Jennings and Jo exchanged looks, and this time he understood she wanted him to answer.

"Judge, the executives can do the heavy lifting *before* the meeting, but the burden of making the presentation would fall to Jo. The lenders want to see her in action, to evaluate her command of facts and strategy. How she presents herself. And to question her about why she wants to change lenders for no appreciable financial gain for her company. At the end of the day, they'll be risking their money as much on *her* as on the company's financial statements."

"A year ago," Jo said, "I would ace an audition like this. But not now. And I've been troubled all along that what we're doing – hiding the ESOP plans from the lenders – was deceptive and dishonest. I talked myself into it because of what was at stake, but I've never done business this way, and I'm actually glad I've been stopped from ending my career this way."

There was no need to further discuss what they all understood. They'd run out of options, and time. Jo's desired outcomes for her employees and her foundation would not happen. Her heart sank when she contemplated possible outcomes. The disposition of her company, her life's work, would now occur in probate, with one of her competitor's being the likely acquirer. She knew early casualties of such transactions would be some or all of her loyal executives – the exact opposite of what she had wanted, planned for, hoped for, and prayed for. And there was the very real possibility that, over time, the company's headquarters would be moved out of Kentucky, ending the jobs and careers of most of her beloved employees.

"Jo," Jennings said, "not for today, but very soon, we need to discuss appointing an interim CEO. Someone to relieve you of the stress you no longer need to take on. I think we're both thinking of the same person, but we also have to give careful thought to the how and why and when to make the leadership change."

She nodded in agreement. The executive they were both thinking of Jo had regarded as her heir-apparent. She was a superb business development executive like her mentor Jo, and she'd worked her way up from an entry-level position fifteen years ago. She knew the company's inner workings across all divisions, and was highly respected, both within and outside the company.

The discussion had completely drained Jo. She hugged Jennings, and thanked him for all he'd done. And for making the drive up. She hugged and kissed her husband, then excused herself.

After a late lunch they barely touched, The Judge and Jo, accompanied by an angel, headed for the eye surgeon's office. After a thorough examination, the doctor's diagnosis was not at all what they had anticipated. Jo's vision problem was indeed related to her SCA, but her eyesight could be completely restored with a fast-acting antibiotic. Jo kept her composure until they were inside the car and pulling away from the medical complex.

Although it was raining, Jo asked that they go for a long drive in the country before returning home. They passed the rest of the afternoon and early evening watching movies at home. Their appetites had returned, and they went to the diner that evening. They were in bed before ten.

Jo called Jennings the next morning. She accepted his offer to manage the entire process of transitioning in the new CEO they both agreed on, and he promised to keep her updated. Setting her cell phone down after the call, Jo reflected on her frustration that she had always prided herself on challenging people to bring her not just problems, but solutions. It was what she had conveyed to Marla when they first discussed the idea of a book months earlier. Now, with her company, and her health, she saw only problems – with no solutions.

But she hadn't gotten where she was by giving up on her dreams, so she continued to pray for her desired outcomes.

I t was early in the first full week of February, and Jo had decided to act on something that had been on her mind since that day after Black Friday – the day she received her SCA prognosis.

"All you have to do is ask," The Judge said

"Well," Jo said, "this request involves you, Charlie and Ruth. And it's very important to me."

"I'm certain all three of us will make it happen. What is it?"

"I want to see the mountains one more time. And snow. There's only a few more months of winter left, and I'd like to go while I still feel up to it. But I obviously can't go alone."

"Nor would I allow it. Not for a minute. And I know Charlie and Ruth would be delighted to go with us to help out."

Their favorite diner had experienced plumbing problems that closed it down for a few days, so they were having an early dinner at a local tavern. For the first time in over twenty years, there was no guardian angel.

A week earlier, Jennings and Lucy Mae had joined The Judge and Jo in a tearful farewell dinner gathering at her Bardstown home for all five angels and their families – people who had become *family* to Jo over the years. The angels were still in the company's employ, but they now served a new CEO. All except for Charlie. He had agreed to delay his retirement plans and work directly for Jo and The Judge in whatever capacity they needed.

"Are you thinking of taking the plane?" The Judge asked.

"I know it sounds selfish, but yes. In all the years we've had a company plane, I've never once used it for a personal trip. But now I don't want to put up with all the hassles, and the uncertainty, of flying commercial to a winter destination."

"I'm sure everyone will understand. And if they don't, you still own the company and it's *your* plane. Besides, no one even needs to know either the purpose or the destination. Your executives can take commercial flights if they need to travel while we're gone."

"I wish it could be just you and me, but it *would* be a great comfort to have Charlie and Ruth along."

"When do you want to leave, and where do you want to go?"

"Where we go is less important than *the when*. I want to leave as soon as possible. Can I leave it to you to choose where we go?"

"You bet. All I need you to do is check and see when we can have the plane."

Their travel plans came together quickly. The plane was available in three days, a Friday, and remarkably, none of the executives were scheduled to travel the following week.

The Judge's first choice was Colorado, and he asked Beverly, Jennings' assistant, to book the accommodations. The only destination that met all their needs on such short notice – mountains, snow, available hotel rooms, and enough runway length for the plane – was Telluride. Beverly booked rooms for The Judge and Jo, for Charlie and Ruth, and one for each of the two pilots.

By ten o'clock Friday morning, they were headed west. Given the Gulfstream's speed and the two-hour time difference, they expected to be in Telluride in time for lunch – if the weather cooperated. It didn't. The Telluride airport is perched somewhat precariously on the side of a mountain and is susceptible to closings due to snowfall or wind. That day, they learned when they were about an hour away that a combination of both meant they had to divert to Denver to wait out the storm.

Charlie searched his cell phone for a number before saying, "I have an idea." Within the span of less than fifteen minutes, Jo's guardian angel had saved the day. Actually, the entire trip.

Charlie and couple of friends had been to Whitefish, Montana the previous summer on a fishing trip. He had made friends with the owner of their hotel and he called him from the plane's phone. After a brief conversation, Charlie asked the man to stay on the phone while he outlined his idea, one Jo and The Judge instantly agreed to. The pilots changed course to the Kalispell airport, where the hotel owner had arranged for two Suburban vehicles to transport them the thirty minutes to Whitefish. When they checked into the hotel, they learned a table for six had been reserved in the lunch room.

In addition to the mountains and snow Jo had sought, their unplanned diversion added the magnificent Whitefish Lake in all its winter splendor. The roads had been cleared of the most recent snowfall, so it was easy for them to be driven to a variety of scenic locations and vistas each morning, returning to town for a leisurely lunch before heading out again in the afternoon. Darkness came early, and the hotel owner's connections enabled them to enjoy dinners at popular local restaurants both Friday and Saturday night.

Jo never really stopped thinking about her business problems, but she did find this escape relaxing. She was even a little surprised when Saturday afternoon Jennings called her cell phone and asked to speak to both her and The Judge. Their hotel room had a speaker phone, so Jo hung up and called him back.

Jennings politely asked about their trip, but Jo and The Judge could sense it wasn't the reason he called. It wasn't.

"I have what I believe is very good news, and I didn't want to wait until you got back. Unless something goes terribly wrong, we've found a way to make the ESOP happen."

"That's fantastic," Jo said, with the most enthusiasm and strength in her voice either man had heard in a long time. "What changed?"

Jennings proceeded to succinctly describe a scenario whereby he would purchase Jo's company – something he could easily do with his financial resources. He would secure the necessary credit line, but without the CEO stipulation that had hamstrung them previously. Once that had been achieved, he would immediately sell the company back to a trust established in Jo's name on the condition the ESOP would be immediately implemented. Jennings went on to explain that if Jo approved the plan, it could all be done relatively quickly and out of the public eye because all entities involved were privately-held.

"Now," Jennings concluded, "I know you need some time to think, so…"

"No," Jo interrupted, "I don't. This is an amazing solution, and I want it done as soon as possible. Can you continue to take care of everything and just send me papers to sign?"

"I can, and I will. One more thing. When you've had a chance to digest all of this, you'll come up with a question that I'm going to answer for you now. All of this was Marla's idea."

"Marla?" Jo and The Judge said in unison.

"I hate to admit it, but we were all so deep in the weeds that we couldn't see the solution that was there all along. When Ben asked her how she came up the idea, and particularly so many of the details, she just said she had been praying for Jo, and it came to her one morning when she was rocking Danielle."

As soon as their call ended, Jo was on the phone with Marla. Both fought back tears as they talked. Their call ended with Jo saying she wanted to get together with Marla as soon as they got home.

At dinner Saturday night, Jo and The Judge shared the news with Charlie and Ruth, and everyone agreed with Jo's suggestion that they fly home the next morning. "But not before we all go to church," Jo insisted. "We have so much to be thankful for."

On the flight home, Jo again thanked The Judge for agreeing to the early return. "I hope you're not disappointed we won't still be in Montana for Valentine's Day next Tuesday, as we planned. I was hoping for it to be such a special day for us."

"Jo, without sounding like a Hallmark card, *every* day we spend together is special. And where we spend our days doesn't matter to me in the least. Besides that, your birthday is coming up in a few weeks."

Thanks to the plane, they were in control of their schedule and arrived back home in Bardstown by early evening. Jo was exhausted, but the experience, and Jennings' call, had created a halo effect of happiness around Jo she hoped she could sustain.

As she rested her head on her pillow, The Judge softly snoring beside her, she wondered if the last few days would mark the end of her travels. That troubling thought kept her from falling asleep until it was replaced by an uplifting one that *did* summon the Sandman.

27

"Question for you."

"Yes."

"Judge, you haven't heard the question."

"Don't need to, Jo. I resolved to myself over my first cup of coffee this morning that I was, henceforth and forever more, never going to say no to you."

After sleeping late, Jo came downstairs the morning after they returned from Montana to find The Judge in the kitchen, reading the Louisville *Courier Journal*. The aroma of freshly-brewed coffee was a wonderful greeting as she entered the room. But a distant second to the hug and kiss.

"Just curious. Is this very moment *henceforth*, or is it *forever more*?"

"Don't know," he replied, with a smile punctuated by a slight shrug to his shoulders. "Don't think it matters. Are you hungry?"

They agreed on cheese omelets and raisin toast, and Jo gathered the ingredients together.

"Back to the question you answered before hearing it. Are you up for another trip?" she asked, hesitantly, refilling his coffee cup.

"Whenever. Wherever. Just say the word."

"Two words. Pawleys Island."

The Judge knew Pawleys was Jo's favorite vacation destination. On the South Carolina coast between Myrtle Beach to the north and Charleston to the south, it had been drawing Jo almost every year since college. The numbers never worked for her to buy a second home there, so she had several homes on a list of preferred rentals.

"When are you thinking? June? July, maybe?"

Pawleys is an oceanfront destination, so The Judge assumed she was thinking of a summer outing.

"Next month."

Jo knew the weather at that time of year was unpredictable, so she suggested they watch the weather forecasts closely. "We can even ask the flight service at Bluegrass to help. As soon as it looks like a few days of great weather, we take off."

"Take off, as in airplane?"

"No. We can drive."

After listening to her husband diplomatically explain why driving would be too arduous for her, and too time-consuming, she said, "Well, I didn't say it was a perfect plan. What do *you* suggest?"

"When the weather cooperates, we charter a small plane that can get us there in an hour or so of flying time. It can either stay with us in South Carolina, or we can order another one when we're ready to come home. Shouldn't cost all that much. And since you provided the wings to Montana, I would insist that this be on me."

"Judge, I just came up with the idea late last night, and in a couple of minutes you have all the details thought through, with a plan that makes complete sense. Ever think about putting that keen mind to good use, like maybe as a trial lawyer?"

"Think I could make a go of it in a courtroom?"

"Don't know. Let me get back to you on that one," she replied, setting his breakfast in front of him.

Rather than beginning to eat, The Judge got up from his stool at the center island, and began changing channels on the small kitchen television.

"Are we done talking?" Jo asked, somewhat perturbed. And this was so unlike him. "What are you doing?"

"Looking for the weather channel."

The third week in March the weather along the South Carolina coast was sunny and unseasonably warm. They checked various sources online to be certain there weren't changes lurking, and the jet leasing company confirmed their finding. The next two weeks, the weather at Pawley's Island looked perfect.

Instead of a small Lear jet, The Judge secured a much roomier Swiss-made Pilatus PC-12 prop plane that could seat nine passengers. It would add a few minutes to their flying time, but they would travel in greater comfort. And since it cost so much less than a jet, he decided the plane would stay with them.

On Saturday, March 24th, Jo, The Judge, Ruth and Charlie arrived at the small Georgetown airport less than twenty minutes south of their destination – Litchfield by the Sea plantation. Jo had previously rented the beach house she'd selected, one inside a gated community and right on the ocean. March was the off-season, so most of her favorite restaurants were still closed for the winter. Just as well, since Ruth, a marvelous cook, had insisted on preparing their meals. Except for breakfast. Jo said that would be her contribution, with The Judge's able assistance.

The second evening they were there, Marla called to say Ben was leaving for Spain the next day, and that Bartolome's parents had agreed for Ben to bring him back with him for a six-day visit that coincided with the boy's spring school break.

"You must be very excited about meeting your grandson," Charlie said, after breakfast the next morning.

"I am," The Judge replied. "It's a surprise, of course. Based on what Ben told me after meeting the adoptive parents, I wasn't expecting to see him until June. Jo, you talked with her. What was Marla's reaction?"

Before answering, Jo quickly processed the options – full disclosure, or partial. She opted for partial.

"Much the same as you. Surprised. Thinking this would all happen months from now."

"Was she excited?" Charlie asked.

Jo had spoken with Marla since returning from Montana, but they had yet to get together. "I'm sure she was. And a little apprehensive." Jo glanced at Ruth with a look she hoped invited intervention, and a change of subject. It worked.

"What's on the agenda today?" Ruth asked.

"I'd like to do a couple of things," Jo said. "I want to take a short walk on the beach. And then drive down to look at the old houses that are actually on Pawleys Island. Many times I thought about buying one. You know, Arrogantly Shabby."

"Arrogantly what?" Charlie asked.

"That's the name given to Pawleys Island," The Judge answered. "Has to do with all the old, rustic houses right on the beach that, if one ever came on the market, would sell for millions."

"Gotta see that," Charlie said. "Ready whenever you folks are."

Charlie accompanied Jo and The Judge on a leisurely walk on the almost deserted beach. They walked slowly, heading south, turning around to retrace their steps after about twenty minutes. Walking in sand is more taxing than a hard surface, and Jo had become very conscious of her limitations.

As soon as they got back to the rental house, Ruth joined them for the ten-minute drive to the narrow bridge that crossed over the marshland leading to Pawleys Island. This area of South Carolina, known as the Low Country, is full of countless species of plants, animals and birds. Jo was wearing a new tee shirt she'd purchased on a previous visit, but never worn. On the back of the shirt, above a rendering of the marshland scenery, dark blue letters read *Marsh Mellow*.

Across the bridge, they took a right turn and drove just a few minutes to the south end of the island, then turned around and drove less than ten minutes to reach the north end. They had quickly accomplished Jo's desire to see the old, "shabby," million-dollar oceanfront houses running the length of the island, and soon headed back onto Highway 17 for lunch at the Litchfield Beach Fish House, one of the few seafood restaurants that had remained open.

Back at the house, Ruth stretched and commented that there really was something seductively relaxing about seeing and hearing the surf. Everyone agreed and they all headed to their respective rooms for naps. Around four, as Ruth and Jo prepared to go outside onto the deck, their companions lined up to join them.

"Nope. Girl time," Ruth said, holding up her hand like a traffic cop.

"What are we supposed to do with 'boy time'?" Charlie asked.

"You'll think of something," his wife answered, as the sliding glass door closed behind them.

Ruth and Jo settled into matching Adirondack chairs, facing the protective sand berm beyond which stretched the vast expanse of the Atlantic Ocean. Looking eastward, Jo realized she would never get to Europe. It had been a dream, but never a priority. Now it was too late.

"Thank you for coming with us. And on such short notice," Jo said, patting her old friend on the arm.

"Charlie and I were delighted to be invited."

"You and Charlie have been so wonderful over the years. Helpful and supportive in more ways than I can count. There's no way I'll ever be able to repay you."

"Jo, Charlie and I love you, and cherish any time we can be together. But Charlie's on your payroll, so he's being paid to be here. And when our times together, yours and mine, have been in my professional capacity, you've always insisted on paying my standard fee. So you see, you can't repay what you've already paid."

"I wasn't talking about money. I hope you know that."

Recovering from her misstep, Ruth said, "I do. I really do. And I'll share a secret with you. If we could have afforded it, my husband would have paid *you*. Working with you has been the highlight of his career."

They continued to talk for an hour or so. About nothing, and everything. The wind was beginning to pick up, so they headed back inside. Both women suppressed their urge to laugh when they found the lawyer and the policeman in the great room, watching re-runs of "Law and Order."

"What time do you want to eat," Ruth asked, as they walked past them on the way to the kitchen.

"Can you give us about thirty minutes?" The Judge asked. "I'd like to finish watching this episode. The lawyers think they have a winnable case. I don't, and I want to see who's right."

Jo rolled her eyes, and Ruth pulled her into the kitchen to continue their conversation.

When they were out of earshot of the men, and had recovered their composure, Jo said, "The Judge is going to indulge me and get up to watch the sunrise. Want to join us?"

"And spoil such a romantic moment for just the two of you? Not a chance. And don't you dare say anything to Charlie, or he'll be there. He'll insist he'll be needed to make sure you don't drown."

"Can't drown if I don't go near the water. And I don't intend to. Just want to see the sunrise."

They were leaving for home the next day, and Ruth worked wonders with the variety of remaining food they'd purchased upon arrival. After a leisurely meal, The Judge asked Jo if she wanted to go down to the community pool area. Not for swimming, he said, but since it was too windy to sit on the beach, to be at the next best water's edge.

Charlie had yet to fully disengage mentally from his years as Jo's bodyguard, and it appeared to Ruth he intended to make it a threesome. She took him aside to gently remind of how things had changed, and motioned for Jo and The Judge to make their exit.

The off-season meant no one else was at the pool. They selected recliner chairs and positioned them so their backs were to the ocean in case the wind came up. The berm was a natural barrier that blocked a view of the ocean, but a gentle breeze did make its way to where they sat, creating enough ripple in the water so that the reflection of the lights illuminating the pool area resembled flickering stars.

Heeding the "No Glass Containers" sign he'd seen earlier, The Judge had emptied half a bottle of New Zealand Cloudy Bay Chardonnay into a plastic container before they left the house. Poolside, he poured it into paper cups. They touched raised cups in a silent toast, then sipped Jo's favorite white wine. A few minutes passed without either of them saying anything.

"Thank you," Jo said.

"You're welcome."

"You might have at least asked 'for what?'" Jo said, her smile so radiant as to belie the battle she was losing internally. "How did you know what I was thinking?"

"I didn't know *exactly*, that's true. But the list of possibilities is endless," he said, again raising his paper cup, "and I wanted to spare you the embarrassment of possibly forgetting one or two. Or more."

"You are *too* kind. How about a summary?" she asked.

"Summarize away. Oh, this may take you some time. Perhaps I should get more wine."

Jo gave him her silent look with full brow-furrowing and nose-wrinkling, trying for feigned disapproval. He played along, unsuccessfully trying to give the appearance of a chastened child who had spoken out of turn. His cup of wine in his left hand, he used his right to give a palm-up gesture for her to continue.

"As I was saying. Or as I was *going* to say," she continued, searching for the words that could best *summarize* her gratitude. Raising her cup, she found the words.

"Mr. Chief Justice Benjamin Taylor, Sr.," was all she got out before he interrupted.

"*Your Honor* also works." Another furrowed brow and wrinkled nose. "I'm sorry, Jo, please continue."

"Honestly, Judge, since you finally got around to proposing to me, I've seen a playful side you've successfully kept hidden. At least from me."

"From everyone. You've brought it out in me. Thank *you*."

"Damn it, Judge. Are we *ever* going to get around to me thanking *you*, which is where this conversation began?"

Jo thought she had her serious face on. He was obviously seeing something else, because he was smiling. But at least he was quiet. Finally.

"What I want to say, what I want you to know…what I want to *thank* you for, is making my dream come true. And in the future, whenever you hear me say thank you, even if it's for holding a door open, or refilling my glass, I want you to *also* imagine hearing me say 'for making my dream come true.' Think you can do that?"

"Yes, I can do that. If you'll do something for me?"

"What?"

"Dance with me."

"Here? Right now?"

"Right here, right now," he said, rising from his recliner and extending his hand to help her do the same.

"We have never once in our entire marriage danced together. Shameful, don't you think?"

"Shameful," she agreed, stepping into his open arms. "What are we going to do for music?"

"I'm going to sing to you."

Jo disengaged, took a step back, and asked. "You can *sing*? I thought all the times we were together in church, you were just mouthing the words because you were self-conscious about your voice."

"Jo, I didn't say I could sing *well*. Or even half-well, if that's a word. But I have a song in mind, one that will just have to do in the absence of the orchestra I would have arranged if I'd known this moment was going to occur."

As she stepped back into his embrace, she asked, "How is it that you know the lyrics of this song you're about to sing?"

"Jo, you had your dreams, and I've had mine. I've often dreamed of this moment, with this song playing in my mind."

With the gentle breeze blowing and the sound of the surf in the background, The Judge waltzed his bride around the deck of a resort swimming pool, softly singing "Could I Have This Dance," a song made popular by Anne Murray.

When they stopped, he stepped back, and took her hands in his.

"Mary Josephine, thank you for making *my* dream come true."

They kissed, gently and for a long time. Jo took him by the hand and as she led him back toward the beach house, she whispered, "Sunrise comes early, and your day, our day, isn't about to end just yet."

28

Ruth was just beginning to make the first pot of morning coffee when she saw The Judge. He was at the top of the stairs at the beach end of a wooden walkway that crossed over the berm. He was carrying a sleeping Jo in his arms, and Ruth thought to herself that they must have gotten up really early to see the sunrise.

Despite his age, Jo's frail condition enabled him to carry her with the same ease as the threshold crossings at the Bardstown residence. As he descended with her into the grassy area between the house and the berm, Charlie, who by this time had joined Ruth in the kitchen, moved to open the wide sliding patio door. It wasn't until The Judge and Jo were inside that Ruth and Charlie realized what had happened. Jo wasn't asleep.

Charlie helped The Judge gently lay Jo on the oversized leather sofa in the living room. Charlie stepped back, and The Judge knelt by her side, carefully smoothing out the white cotton sun dress she was wearing. He straightened her arms, then placed the palm of her right hand on top of her left. He leaned forward and kissed her lightly on the forehead. Standing, he patted Charlie's shoulder as he passed silently in front of him, and walked back out the door.

Ruth and Charlie watched him cross over the walkway until he descended onto the beach and out of sight. Concerned, Charlie followed, but was still on the walkway when The Judge appeared at the top of the stairs on his way back. In his left hand were Jo's sandals. As he stepped onto the walkway, he wavered slightly, and Charlie rushed toward him. But the older man had already steadied himself with his right hand on the railing by the time Jo's final guardian angel reached him. With The Judge's right arm around Charlie's shoulder, the two men slowly, and wordlessly, returned to the house.

Back inside, The Judge returned to kneel beside Jo, taking her hands in his. As Charlie began to close the sliding door, The Judge finally spoke.

"Please leave it open. Jo loved the sound of ocean, and the tide's coming in."

With Charlie now standing at her side, Ruth squeezed his hand, and he followed her lead as they both sat down on the floor a respect-ful distance away. They were now looking up at The Judge as he began to speak, his eyes remaining on Jo.

"We set an alarm to be on the beach while it was still dark. It was low tide, so the water was maybe thirty yards away. As it started get-ting light, Jo wanted to feel the ocean again. We took off our shoes, and walked out to the water's edge. She said the sun rising above the ocean was just how she wanted to remember it."

He paused, the sound of the ocean filling the void.

"The tide was coming in, higher and higher on our legs. When she decided it was time to turn around and go back, we noticed our shadows on the sand. Jo said she wanted there to be just one, and hugged me until it happened. We headed toward the house, but when we reached the walkway, she asked if we could stay a while longer. We sat down, and leaned against the berm like it was a beach chair."

The ocean sounds again filled the room. The Judge turned his head toward them.

"Jo began talking about what she was seeing and feeling, and hearing. She said it would help her commit everything to memory. Like *the gentle swaying of the sea oats in the breeze coming from the south.*

The heaviness of salt air. The sounds of seagulls passing overhead. The Sandpipers searching for the breakfast the incoming tide served up. Her words were so descriptive, but her voice was getting weaker."

He looked at Jo for a few seconds, then turned toward them again.

"When she closed her eyes, I thought it was to strengthen her memory of what she was experiencing. She rested her head on my shoulder, and I moved a little to better support her. She opened her eyes, smiled, and said 'Thank you.' And then she was gone."

The sound of both Ruth and Charlie crying mixed with the ocean tide.

"If I could, I would have stayed there with her forever. To have that moment never end. But I heard voices in the distance, and knew I couldn't let her be seen by strangers."

The celebration of her life took place at Jo's church in Versailles the following Saturday. The temperature was expected to reach seventy by mid-day, and there wasn't a cloud in the sky. Spring in all its glory had come to Jo's beloved Kentucky.

Marla had heard of the church Jo attended, but had never been. It was one of those mega-churches, and as the hour of the service approached, almost every one of the 2,000 seats in the sanctuary was filled. Jo's employees and their families were by far the largest contingent, along with a large number of executives and employees of Jennings' many companies. Local and state officials came because of her company's economic contribution to a state struggling to find new directions away from reliance upon tobacco and coal.

The marriage of the retiring Chief Justice to the state's most successful businesswoman had received a lot of press coverage, and that brought many who had either a personal or professional relationship with The Judge. With her prior approval, Jo's death ended the anonymity of her substantial charitable giving, so following her company's public disclosure, the grateful recipient organizations were represented. And, of course, members of the church.

The program had been structured in three parts — the past, the present, and the future.

Jennings spoke of the *past*, from Jo's birth until she left his company to start her own. Madelyn Cunningham, the company's new CEO, spoke of the *present*, succinctly tracing Jo's success from the company's beginning to her surprise announcement that Jo's companies would soon be owned by her employees. She said details would be forthcoming soon, and as the announcement was being digested, especially by Jo's employees and their families, there was faint whispering that ended quickly as Marla approached the podium.

29

"Mary Josephine Gilpin was my friend," Marla began, nervously. "And for the last few months of her life, we were both Mrs. Taylor because she married my husband's father. I was honored when I learned Jo had asked me to speak to you."

Marla said that while Jo would be humbled by the overwhelming turnout to celebrate her life, she knew she would be pleased so many people important to her were gathered together. The longer she spoke, the more comfortable she became, with her voice becoming stronger and more assured.

"Madelyn told you about the ownership change of Jo's company so that I could tell you this. All the proceeds of the sale will go to a foundation Jo created that has two missions – sickle-cell anemia research and helping at-risk children in her beloved state of Kentucky. Her advocacy for these children for decades came from compassion, not pity. And she was also committed to the pursuit of a cure for the disease that claimed her life, and that of her mother and her first husband." Marla's voice cracked with emotion when she added, "And I was humbled when Jo asked me to be president of her foundation."

After pausing to regain her composure, Marla said, "I've read that true greatness is measured by what is done for those who can't reciprocate. Jo knew during the last year of her life what almost no one else knew. That it would *be* her last. Yet until almost the very end, she remained involved in stressful activities that enabled what's been shared with you this morning. Jo would never have anointed herself with a mantle of greatness, but all of us know she surely was. I only wish we had the time this morning to count all the ways.

I could cast aside my prepared remarks and, like many of you, talk endlessly about the most remarkable woman I've ever known. And, *remarkably*, I only met Jo last August. Such was her impact on me, and on my life. Your presence here speaks to her influence on *your* life. I now want to share with you what brought Jo and me together for the first time two hundred and twenty-six days ago.

We all know that most of what is said here today may be forgotten tomorrow. But Jo's own words will live on because she wrote a book that will be published next week. *Her* thoughts, in *her* own words. Forever. In preparing for today, I listened to every taped conversation I had with Jo as we worked together on her book for the past several months. I believe she would approve of my selection."

At that moment, the recording of Jo's voice was heard through the sanctuary's sound system:

I've known since college that my illness meant a day would come in my twenties when my yesterdays would begin to exceed my tomorrows. But my first husband, Barrey Kelly, who also had SCA, taught me about living, and dying. When Barrey died, I chose to try to live each day so that if it became my last, I would be proud of all that I had said, and done, that day. Was I always successful? Of course not. But I always tried.

Marla waited for a few moments for many of those assembled to compose themselves after hearing Jo's voice, then continued.

"Mary Josephine Gilpin Kelly Taylor listened to her mother, who told her *dreams never come true for those who never dream.* Jo followed her dreams, and took many of us along with her. She will be long remembered, but not with a monument in a cemetery. There won't be one because she insisted that there not be. But we all have her in our hearts. Thank you for coming. Please don't hurry away. Stay, and have fellowship with others whose lives were also touched by the wonderful woman who brought us together today."

A week later, at Jennings' request, there was a gathering on Park Row. The Judge, Lucy Mae, Beverly, Charlie and Ruth, Marla and Ben were all seated in the spacious living room of the upstairs residence.

"Things happened so fast the last couple of weeks that The Judge and I thought it would be a good idea to get everyone together. The first order of business is for us to again thank Marla for her inspired idea that enabled both the ESOP and the funding of Jo's foundation."

"That's very kind of you, Jennings," Marla said, "but all of you know where the idea came from. My contribution was lifting Jo's burdens up in prayer, and opening my mind and my heart for the inspiration that I hoped would come."

"Marla," Ruth said, "I think we all have the same question for you. The book. Jo's book. What happened? It hadn't been mentioned for a long time, and I, for one, assumed it wasn't going to happen."

"When Jo got her prognosis the day after Thanksgiving," Marla answered, "our book discussions ended. Then she completely surprised me weeks later with a call. It was while Ben was in Spain the first time. She said she had an idea for a book much different than I had proposed – and that I had been working on. When she described what she was thinking, I thought it was a great idea, and one we could complete in a very short timeframe. *And,* she had recruited someone without whom it wouldn't have happened."

"Who was that?" Ben asked. He was aware Marla had continued working on the book with Jo, but assumed it was just the two of them.

"Your father," Marla answered, then turned to in the direction of their recruit and said, "Judge, please take it from here."

"Oh, there's not much to say, really. Jo's eyesight was beginning to be a problem, as was her stamina. I just helped out when I could."

"It would come as no surprise to all of you that The Judge is minimizing his contribution," Marla said. "Everything came together quickly and, I might add, beautifully. Don't you think so, Judge?"

"I do."

"We had selected a publisher months earlier," Marla told them, "and they were incredibly supportive in working with the aggressive timeline we wanted."

"I need to say this," The Judge said. "That timeline was being driven by what we thought was Jo's failing eyesight, not any anticipation her end was near. Our goal, hers and mine, was for her to be with you one more Christmas."

The room became silent for several seconds before Beverly spoke. "Marla, when will the book be available? I can't wait to read it."

"Can you wait two minutes?" The Judge asked.

"Absolutely!"

He excused himself, returning with a sealed box and a knife.

"Before we left for South Carolina," he said, beginning to cut the tape, "Jo had advance copies delivered to Bardstown so she could inscribe a personal note for each us. When she finished, she taped the box shut. I haven't seen anything she wrote."

One by one, The Judge removed the books and handed them out based upon Jo's inscription. They read in silence, save for the occasional sniffle at something she wrote. After everyone closed their books, it was Lucy Mae who asked, "Marla, how did you select the name *My Way*?"

"I didn't. Jo did."

"Because of the song?" Ruth asked.

"No." Marla answered. "You'll understand when you read the book. But I did research the song, and learned it was recorded by Frank Sinatra before I was born."

"And a lot of people, especially fans like me, associate it with Elvis," Charlie added.

"Right," Marla confirmed. "I learned he picked it up several years later. But it was Jo who told me about a friend of both men – a Welsh singer I'd never heard of by the name of Shirley Bassey. I looked her up on You Tube. She's fantastic! And she only had to change a couple of words to make the song's lyrics relevant to women."

"Is there any way we can see it?" Lucy Mae asked.

"There is," Ben answered, getting up and moving to the entertainment center. It took him a few minutes, but he was successful in calling up the You Tube display of various video postings of Shirley Bassey. Marla selected one in particular, and Ben brought it to life on their widescreen television.

Watching their reactions, it was obvious to Marla it had the same impact on everyone else that it had the first time she saw it. For two reasons. Her powerfully beautiful rendition of a familiar song written by Paul Anka. *And* her uncanny resemblance to Jo. For even though she was from Wales, her father was Nigerian. She was, like Jo, a stunningly beautiful woman of color.

"I wasn't ready for that!' Ruth said.

"I don't think any of us were," Charlie added. "Judge, had you seen this before?"

"Yes. Jo and I watched it together several times as we worked on the book."

"Now to the primary reason we wanted all of you to be with us today," Jennings said. "As you know, it was Jo's wish to be cremated, and she didn't want a monument." He turned and looked at The Judge.

"Jo passed away sooner than any of us anticipated," The Judge said, "and she never said what she wanted done with her ashes.

Jennings and I talked about it, and we hope you'll be pleased with our decision. Please join us for a change of venue."

Less than twenty minutes later, they were at the gravesite of Jo's mother in Bowling Green's Fairview Cemetery. Cynthia Dara Gilpin's monument was positioned on the right side of a two-plot site, and on the left side there was a green cloth on the ground next to a small pile of dirt.

The Judge and Jennings had kept their *no monument* promise, and found a way to return Jo to her mother's side.

FIN

My Way

M. Josephine Gilpin

Dedication

This book is dedicated to my True North.

Table of Contents

Forward

*"Books say: She did this because. Life says: She
did this. Books are where things are explained
to you; life is where things aren't. I'm not
surprised some people prefer books."*

— JULIAN BARNES

MARY JOSEPHINE GILPIN WAS THE most remarkable woman I've ever
met, yet we'd only known each other for 219 days when she died.

Jo was arguably Kentucky's most successful woman entrepreneur,
and certainly one of its leading philanthropists. In our first meeting,
I asked what she felt was the one thing most responsible for her success. She said it was the decades-long mentoring from one of the
South's leading businessmen – and their shared commitment to keeping journals.

Listening to her, I intuitively thought her journals could help others, primarily women, on their life journey, and I asked if I could
read them. She reluctantly agreed, and my enthusiasm for a journals-
to-book initiative grew the more I read. When I finished, I was con-
vinced the content was truly inspirational, yet the amount and variety

1

of the journal entries was daunting. I was a few months into the organizing process when we learned Jo was losing her battle with an illness first diagnosed when she was a young girl. By then, Jo had become committed to the book idea, but we both knew we were running out of time.

Early on, Jo asked me what we wanted to achieve. I had initially envisioned writing a book about her – an idea she immediately rejected. She felt that the practice of journaling – so important to her and to her mentor – should be encouraged, and it became the book's foundation. And it was Jo who suggested we address gender inequality because, in her words, "It's the sun around which so many other women's issues orbit."

As a professional writing coach and editor, my contribution was limited to guiding a first-time author. Because we recorded our conversations, the words are all Jo's. The phrases and quotes shown in bold type are lifted directly from her journal entries. Although it would be an intimate look into her journals, Jo was adamant that the book not be about her, rather a conversation with her readers about *them*. You'll begin to understand as soon as you turn to the next page.

Jo wanted me to be listed as the author. I disagreed, and I prevailed. What we did agree upon at the outset was that all income would go to her foundation for the benefit of others.

Jo lived long enough to see *My Way* published. She inscribed a personalized message in one for me, and it will always be among my most treasured possessions. It was Jo who selected the book's title, and we both hope when you're finished reading, it will become *your* way.

Marla Jo Taylor

Introduction

*"Build your own dreams, or someone else will
hire you to build theirs."*

– FARRAH GRAY

"MY" IN *MY WAY* REFERS not to me, rather to every woman or man who reads this book. It was written for you. All I ask you to do is to open your mind – and your heart.

The phrases in **bold italics** are not mine, but at different times, and in different ways, they lifted me up and helped take me from where I was to where I wanted to be. I hope some of them will do the same for you.

We've all heard success is a journey, not a destination. What I've shared are some of the stepping stones that carried me on my journey – down a road always under construction, past detours and frustrating delays, accidents and dead ends.

Ever since I was a little girl, I've cut out articles from newspapers, magazines and other publications that touched me in a special way.

My first clipping was from the cover of a church bulletin. It said: **Never be afraid to trust an unknown future to a known God.**

Beginning that day long ago, I wrote down thoughtful, insightful or inspiring statements I read or heard. I always tried to have pen and paper with me everywhere I went, taking notes of what I heard in speeches and sermons, and in all manner of presentations and interactions. I also wrote down my own thoughts that were inspired by those of others.

These two activities combined to create journals for my personal use, and it was impossible for me to place a value on them. I would have been lost, at times, without them. I hope you can be persuaded to create journals of your own.

Is this a self-improvement book? I certainly hope so. After reading mine, I hope you'll be motivated to head to the nearest bookstore, or go online, and search for the works of other authors in the genre. They'll make great gifts to the most important person in your life – you.

Unfortunately, these wonderful books, once read, are often set aside and never accessed again. Instead of relying on books written by others, if you will follow my lead, you'll be writing your own, and it will virtually assure that *your* book will never gather dust. It will be comprised of both your words, and the words of others who have inspired you. Hopefully, it will become second nature to you because:

"Make good habits, and they will make you."

– Parks Cousins

With a little practice and a lot of commitment, this shouldn't be difficult. But if it is, don't worry, because, as John Norley said:

4

"Most new things are difficult before they are easy."

Creating this book wasn't my idea. When I agreed, I thought it would focus solely on the content of my journals. But the publishing professionals said the messages we wanted to convey would be evaluated by readers based upon the credibility of the messenger, so it would be important for you to know how successful I was in applying what I'm sharing.

So, who am I? What is my story, and why should you care what I have to say and to share? I was persuaded by people I trust that it's because many women, and especially women of color, can relate to my life's journey and benefit from my experiences. My collaborator Marla Taylor and I hope you'll learn from my failures and my successes and chart a course to realize *your* dreams in less time and with less hardship. Or as the outspoken actress Tallulah Bankhead once said:

"If I had to live my life over again, I'd make the same mistakes, only sooner."

I never knew my father, and the circumstances are unimportant. I found out much later he died a few years after I was born, killed in combat serving our country in faraway Vietnam. Living in Bowling Green, Kentucky, my mother worked hard to provide for us. We never wanted for the essentials, and anything else was unimportant because of our love for each other.

When I was nine years old, I saw a televised replay of Martin Luther King's *I Have A Dream* speech delivered on the steps of the Lincoln Memorial. I was mesmerized, committing his inspirational words to memory and reciting them in my mind every night until I fell asleep.

And I focused on *my* dreams. What I wanted to accomplish with my life. The person I saw myself becoming. What I wanted to do for myself, and for others. One afternoon, I asked my mother if it was wrong for me to have such big dreams, since I would have to travel so very far, in so many ways, in order to realize them. Her loving answer contained the most important words ever spoken to me:

"Dreams never come true for those who never dream."

– CYNTHIA DARA GILPIN

I earned an academic scholarship to Western Kentucky University. After graduation, one of the South's most successful entrepreneurs offered me a coveted entry-level management trainee position with one of his companies. I was grateful, but my biggest dream was to create my own company, and for that I knew I needed sales experience. So instead, I asked for an outside sales position. The job was extremely challenging, but I worked hard and consistently exceeded the company's expectations – and mine.

After a few years, my employer offered a small loan to get me started with my own company. It was a scary time for me, but that loan, which was paid back in full, and quickly, was not nearly as important as the mentor relationship that accompanied it. I discovered he kept journals of his own, and we often discussed what we'd seen, heard or read that had made an impact on us. To this day, despite being of different generations, he remains not only my closest business adviser and confidant, but also one of my dearest friends.

Careful research led me to start a manufacturing company to broaden the selection of cosmetics available to African-American women. Many years later, we expanded into the production of environmentally-sensitive cleaning products. I love my home state of

Kentucky, so I located my first small facility here and never gave any thought of going elsewhere as we continued to grow.

My journey had its challenges, both small and large, and there were times when I felt terribly alone and inadequate to meet those challenges. But with a wonderful team of executives and employees over the years, we grew and prospered, and the result is what you may recognize as Hiva Erlene cosmetics and One World cleaning products, which are sold nationwide.

As the sole shareholder, I never once considered taking the company public, merging it or selling it. I was concerned what the loss of my control of the company might mean for my employees' future – the people without whom none of what had been achieved would have been possible. At my direction, the company transitioned to employee-owned through an Employee Stock Ownership Plan (ESOP), and I ended any company involvement. I had realized my dream; I wanted my employees to realize theirs.

We had been very disciplined and paid attention to the fundamentals. But we were also opportunistic and took calculated risks. It's a matter of public record that the company I founded with $10,000 of borrowed money in 1991 had a $287 million valuation when the ESOP transition occurred in early 2017.

That said, I'm always concerned when individual achievements are measured in terms of money, position, power, prestige, recognition and so forth. In my life, I tried, although not always successfully, to be guided by the words of John Ruskin:

> *"The highest reward for a person's toil is not what they get for it, but what they become by it."*

Not everything you read in the coming pages will be new for you. Likely, you've previously heard or read some of what I've shared, though perhaps I've expressed it in a different way. Regardless, your reading the words and phrases again, and embracing some of them as you deem appropriate in your life, will have made my labor of love all worthwhile.

Can just a few words be life-changing? Of course they can. They've toppled oppressive governments, collapsed walls that divided international cities, and put Americans on the lunar surface. They can break our hearts, or take us to unimagined heights of professional achievement and personal happiness. Words can inspire us, cause us to look deep within ourselves, and to look differently at the world around us. And as words move us, we can also become inspired to move others in a positive way.

Marla and I agreed that the way for you to read our book, or any book of its kind, is to think about the next person you'll share it with. As you read, you're encouraged to make liberal use of a highlighter pen, and pen or pencil.

My hope is that you will be inspired to begin your own journal before you finish reading, and nothing would please me more than for passages in this book to touch you in a way that will enable you to achieve your goals, and live life to its fullest – as envisioned by *you*.

I shared with you my mother's answer to my question about dreams. Years later, I read this unattributed quotation:

Little girls with dreams often become women with vision.

I believe with all my heart that if I can, so can you. The time has now come for you to:

Dream, and make those dreams come true.

The Idea

"There is one thing stronger than all the armies
of the world – an idea whose time has come."

– VICTOR HUGO

GREAT LEADERS ARTICULATE VISIONS THAT at the time sounded like dreams – a man on the moon in less than ten years, equal rights for all citizens, an entrepreneur's innovative idea. And dreams they remained until there was a disciplined follow-through, with attention to all the details necessary to enable them to become reality, because: ***Vision without discipline is a dream.***

Simply stated, the idea I'm proposing is for you to embrace the practice of keeping journals to create that discipline in your life. If you do, your journals will have the words and phrases of others that resonate with you, as well as your own thoughts and ideas because:

"If your life is worth living, it's worth recording."

– MARILYN GREY

I urge you to keep *My Way* as the title of your journal collection, and to have the discipline to make at least one journal entry every week.

The world around us moves at such speed, and with such complexity, as to overwhelm all of us from time to time, and no one person has all the answers for dealing with life's challenges. But since these challenges are unique to each and every individual, journaling can be one answer that is, by design, also individually unique.

Your *My Way* journal will be a one-of-a-kind repository, and an easy-to-maintain framework for collection, organization, retention and re-visiting. Mine began as school notebooks into which I pasted things I cut out of magazines and newspapers, as well as my own handwritten thoughts. Because the entries were chronological, they were not organized by subject. That came years later with technology. How you begin, and how your journaling may change over time, is entirely up to you. There are even "how to" books written about journaling. The only thing truly important is that you begin – and that you continue.

The ***bold italics*** words you'll read are only a few examples of what I accumulated during my more than thirty-year commitment to journaling. They are the thoughts of others that inspired me, centered me, focused me, and directed me in both my personal and professional life. I've shared their words as journaling examples, of course, but also in anticipation that some of them will touch you in a special way.

Because I wanted *My Way* to be focused on you, I knew you wouldn't agree with everything I've written. And that's the way it should be. What's important is for you to become comfortable with internalizing the words and phrases of others that you, and you alone, select for inclusion in *your* journals. And by adding your own thoughts, you will write your own book and not rely solely upon books written by authors who have no direct connection to your life. As you do, remember:

"Pale ink is better than the most retentive memory."

— UNKNOWN

I believe that just knowing about journaling is valuable, even if the practice isn't immediately taken up, because in the words of Justice Oliver Wendell Holmes:

"A person's mind, once stretched to a new idea, never regains its original dimensions."

Brevity and Simplicity

*"We do not remember days, we remember
moments."*

– CESARE PAVESE

I BEGAN MY JOURNALS AS a young child, and they were simple. As an adult, my entries became longer and longer, with the thoughts they conveyed growing in complexity. Sentences became paragraphs, and I found myself returning less frequently to the journals, with their value to me diminishing over time. I had forgotten one of the entries from my college days that said:

*62% of all ideas are accepted after being heard, read or
repeated at least six times. The briefer and simpler the
conveyance of a message, the greater the likelihood it will
find a pathway into my life.*

Fortunately, I mentioned my frustration to my mentor, and he showed me one of the entries in *his* journal. It said there are only 26 letters, 10 numbers, 7 basic musical notes and 3 primary colors (red, blue and yellow). That one simple sentence spoke volumes to me.

He then showed me an entry that listed word counts:

400 – The account of creation, found in the book of Genesis
286 – Abraham Lincoln's Gettysburg Address
179 – The Ten Commandments
66 – The Lord's Prayer

I immediately understood both the beauty and the effectiveness in the brevity of those four selections. Together, they've been read by billions of people over time, with the last two memorized by hundreds of millions. From that moment on, *simple is good* and *brief is better* once again became my mantra for journal entries.

One of the most captivating Christmas books ever written was *The Gift of the Magi* by O. Henry. If you re-read it, or read for the first time, it won't take you long – it's only 2,163 words.

I believe one of the most inspiring speeches ever given was delivered by Apple co-founder Steve Jobs in just fifteen minutes at the 2005 Stanford University commencement ceremony. The video is available on You Tube, and the text can easily be found online.

Now-retired evangelist Billy Graham is widely acknowledged as one of the world's greatest preachers. For decades, he spoke at events with tens of thousands of people in attendance. Although those assembled would have listened attentively for as long as he chose to speak, his sermons usually lasted only fifteen minutes.

Were those in the audience at Stanford that summer day, or at the hundreds of Billy Graham Crusades over the years, in any way cheated by the brevity of the speakers? As of this writing, the Jobs' speech has been viewed over 27 million times on You Tube. Reverend Graham continued to pack stadiums all over the world for decades, even though those attending could barely see him at the venue and knew that he would likely speak for only a quarter-hour.

I believe country music songwriters are some of the world's greatest poets and storytellers. Their few words can capture a listener in seconds, and unfold an entire story of wondrous joy or painful heartbreak in less than three minutes. And the brief lyrics of Bob Dylan's songs earned for him the 2017 Noble Prize for Literature.

Brevity and simplicity have worked for others, and they'll work for you.

Truth and Honesty

"If I lie to myself, I've harmed the most
important person in the world."

– UNKNOWN

MY JOURNALS HELPED ME REMAIN centered and focused as I pursued my dreams and tried to live my life *My Way*. That may sound selfish, and it is, but if we don't take control of our own lives, others will. The more entries I made in my journals, the more I came to understand that in order for my dreams to come true, I should: ***Be myself, but be my best self.***

Many of my entries pertained to the need for me to be honest with myself first, and then others. And part of that honesty was acceptance that I could not mold reality to my personal circumstances, because: ***Truth is truth, regardless of what I think or choose to believe.***

Being honest with myself was important when confronted with unpleasant events or circumstances because I needed to understand the difference between what actually happened, and what I thought happened. I have re-read this journal entry many times:

*"It's not what happens to you, but how you react
to it that matters."*

– Epictetus

Since life is not always as we would want it to be, I believe honesty
requires accepting something I heard in one of the very best sales
training classes I attended:

"Pain is inevitable, but misery is a choice."

– Adrienne Albert

When we're honest with ourselves, and others, the world takes notice.
As it does when we fail the test of honesty, because as Ralph Waldo
Emerson said:

"Who you are speaks so loudly I can't hear what you say."

In quiet places, and in quiet times of my choosing, I often reminded
myself of a growing list of things I honestly believed about myself
and my life. In one of those reflective moments, I recalled this journal entry: ***It makes no sense for me to desire incompatible things
or outcomes.***

Something we've all probably learned from experience in everyday
life***: If I tell the truth, I don't have to remember what I say. Otherwise,
I'll need a great memory.***

We all realized early in life that not everyone will like us, and that
was certainly true for me. But we *can* strive to behave in such a way
that others would respect us. For me, this began with telling the truth,

and living up to my words, because: ***I am my word. If it's no good, then neither am I.***

I knew it was imperative that I respect myself at all times because: ***If I don't respect myself and what I'm doing with my life, no one else will.***

Early in my sales career, I was sitting in the office of a successful businessman. I committed to memory, and later wrote in my journals, this saying he had framed on the wall behind his desk: ***Ethics is obedience to the unenforceable, and integrity is adherence to ethics.***

Happiness

"Happiness is a direction, not a place."

— UNKNOWN

IT WAS AT MY UNHAPPIEST times that I turned most often to my journals, and one entry in particular helped get me back on track. It said: **We can be as happy, or as unhappy, as we make up our minds to be.**

Once during my travels, I visited a church in a small town and wrote down on the program these words from the pastor's sermon:

"Don't seek happiness in the future; seek it today and every day."

I almost always kept my feelings of unhappiness to myself, playing things over and over in my mind, not always being aware that worry is rooted in memory. Looking back, most things I worried about, and made myself unhappy over, never happened. As a person of faith, I often had to remind myself that: ***Worry is a misuse of imagination, and is actually prayer in reverse***.

I do remember one specific time when the words of Byron Katie snapped me out of an unpleasant conversation I was having with myself:

> *"Don't believe everything you think."*

And it was very comforting to re-read from time to time that: **My brain may deceive me, but my heart will whisper the truth. I will listen for it.**

Looking back, the times when I was unhappy often coincided with being focused entirely on myself and my priorities, forgetting that Martin Luther King said:

> *"Life's most persistent and urgent question is: What are you doing for others?"*

In Journal 3 I mentioned selfishness in controlling my personal destiny, my journey. But this was not to the exclusion of being an activist for change that impacts others. I can't count the number of times I brought happiness into my life by helping others, even in the smallest ways, knowing:

> *"It is one of the beautiful compensations in this life that no one can sincerely try to help another without helping himself."*
>
> – RALPH WALDO EMERSON

And happiness can come from helping others in non-material ways, since:

> *"There is more hunger for love and appreciation*
> *in this world than for bread."*
>
> **– MOTHER TERESA**

You may have discovered as I did that we are likely to be happiest when we feel good about ourselves – physically. Eating healthy and engaging in regular and rigorous exercise can bring truth to the phrase: **Mental fitness and a healthy body are usually found together.**

I believe the best way for anyone to live a happy life is to ask for help in times of need, or as Carrie Westington said:

> *"At day's end, I turn my problems over to God. He's going*
> *to be up all night anyway."*

JOURNAL 5

Life Isn't Fair

"Life is what we make it. Always has been,
always will be."

– GRANDMA MOSES

LIFE ISN'T FAIR – IT **never has been, and it never will be** is a lesson
I'm grateful I learned very early on. When I graduated from college
over thirty-five years ago, I would have never guessed that in 2016,
and for the foreseeable future, women will, generally speaking, have
fewer advantages in the workplace than their male counterparts with
similar education, age, experience and training. Again, *generally speak-*
ing, they will earn less, advance less quickly and with less certainty. Life
isn't fair.

Everyone has heard of the glass ceiling, and many have experienced it. There is also the seldom-discussed "glass cliff" phenom-
enon, which occurs when women are more likely than men to accept
opportunities to lead companies in distress or crisis as their way to
break C-Suite glass ceilings. These choices often result in women
executives setting themselves up for inevitable failure, the same fate
that would likely occur to any man who had accepted the position at

the same time under the same circumstances. But the woman executive would likely be judged more harshly for her failure. Life isn't fair.

Being underpaid for their efforts, and disproportionately punished for their failings, is a reality for women in the upper reaches of corporate America, and elsewhere, with men and women encountering different expectations regarding workplace risk and reward. Life isn't fair.

The choices, and resulting sacrifices, for men and women regarding the responsibilities of family and children are not the same. Men are seldom limited in their career choices by these responsibilities. Women often are. Life isn't fair.

Overt gender bias may be on the decline in the United States, and in other countries, but implicit and institutional bias remains. Women of color, in addition to gender bias, experience a multiplier effect to their challenges. It's a sad reality, but a reality nonetheless. Life isn't fair.

Although the unfairness is a reality, it must not remain unchallenged, because: ***Not everything faced can be changed. But nothing can be changed until faced.***

And, thankfully, another reality is that: ***The only thing permanent is change.***

As solutions to gender equality are explored, please remember: ***We are continually faced with great opportunities brilliantly disguised as unsolvable problems.***

I believe the beginning point for effecting change in our lives is to remember:

> ***"Destiny is not a matter of chance. It's a matter of choice."***
>
> **– UNKNOWN**

JOURNAL 6

Choices

*"We are where we are in life because that's
where we've chosen to be."*

– UNKNOWN

THERE ARE LIMITATIONS ON ALL of us, of course, but in America, and in most circumstances, we usually have the ability to choose what will and will not impact our lives, and our dreams, because: ***Our greatest power is the free exercise of choice.***

Even as a teenager, I learned that with that power came responsibility, since: ***There will be occasions when we have to choose between what we believe is right, and what we suspect is advantageous.***

I also learned that: ***Knowing what's right, and doing it, are two entirely different things.*** I would never say I always did the right thing, but I think I tried as often as possible.

In my life, my choices were almost always directly connected to both the positive results I achieved and the disappointments I endured, so: **Making wise choices reduces the necessity of taking chances.**

23

There were many times in my professional and personal life when I masterfully accomplished the tasks associated with the *wrong* choices, instead of stumbling while attempting to succeed with the *right* choices. If that has been true in your life, please be mindful of: **Doing the right things, rather than doing things right.**

Like you, I had my fair share of failures and disappointments. But most of my choices turned out just fine, and I want to share a couple of them with you. The first was to be the florist in my life, structuring my priorities as if they were properly arranged flowers. If you agree, then this means, of course, that you will first focus on yourself and your dreams before concerning yourself with the individual or collective dreams of others. Reasoning by analogy, it's somewhat like the flight attendant's instruction to secure your own oxygen mask first.

The second choice involves your response to gender inequality. You can invest time in online searches and read the plethora of available books to empirically confirm the unfairness, the ugliness, the disparity. And then agonize over the results you *knew* you were going to find. Which to me makes about as much sense as a warrior general visiting the severely wounded in a field hospital to seek inspiration before advancing her remaining soldiers into battle.

I encourage you to decide that this reality will *not* continue to apply to you. If you do, you can thoughtfully and methodically prepare as fully as possible to change your personal circumstances, and those things you *can* directly impact, that are standing between you and the realization of your dreams, because: **My uniqueness can be my passport to success, but it's entirely up to me.**

If you agree with me about the futility of reading about problems in the absence of a credible discussion of solutions, and if you accept the necessity of first fitting your own oxygen mask before helping others, the next step will be to: ***Manage to the result I wish to achieve.***

The key, of course, is knowing what you want to achieve professionally, and in what timeframe. Then select from among the available choices, encouraged by the thinking that:

> *"The pessimist sees the difficulty in every opportunity; the optimist sees the opportunity in every difficulty."*

> *– L.P. JACKS*

You can join me and take the entrepreneurial leap. It will give you the greatest possible control over your destiny and the realization of your dreams. Risky? Of course. But I've always believed: ***The only thing worse than taking a risk, and not succeeding, is not taking a risk.***

In stepping out as an entrepreneur, you will soon learn the value of taking intelligent risks. This will involve a pursuit grounded in real possibilities for success based upon knowledge, preparation, desire and your belief in the value of achieving the ultimate outcome, all the while acknowledging: ***Nothing ventured, nothing gained.***

A second choice would be to pursue a new career, or a new direction within your existing career, with companies that have proven over time to have a more sustainably favorable environment for women in terms of performance-based income equality and advancement opportunities. In this way: ***Instead of being a victim of circumstance, I will make my own circumstances.***

A third choice would be to remain with your current employer but navigate away from a position that limits you, charting a course correction more aligned with the fulfillment of your professional dreams. This may involve a step backward or a lateral move, a delay in promotion potential or a merit-based compensation increase, but you understand it's the end result you need to focus on. It may take you out of your "comfort zone," but: ***The road to success begins where my comfort zone ends.***

Before you make this choice, I encourage you to be guided by the thinking that: ***It's equality of opportunity, not equality of condition, I desire.***

Fourth, you could decide to remain where you are and begin to professionally and appropriately challenge your employer's workplace unfairness. Only you will know what that path might look like, and the probability of desirable outcomes. It will take courage, but: ***Courage is often seen as the opposite of conformity.***

Fifth, you could choose to pursue a career path that places you in an environment with virtual certainty of significant gender-based problems. These industries and institutions are well-known, and they have not been completely without positive career improvements for women. If this is the direction of your dreams, it should be pursued with a careful risk/reward assessment, as well as an understanding of a realistic timeframe for achievement. But unless you achieve an unfettered leadership position, your challenge will be how to: ***Influence, without influence.***

Finally, the last option from what I believe are your available choices is to remain where you are. This means you will need to wait for events outside your control, or for the actions of others, to remove the obstacles and pave the way for your journey toward the realization of your dreams. And you must understand this choice will not be free of consequences, because: ***No decision will have its own result.***

If your choice is not to personally "lean in" to the headwinds of workplace gender adversity, it does not mean you cannot, and should not, find ways to be meaningfully supportive of those who have chosen to take to that field of battle – in the legislatures, in the courts, and in the exercise of free speech and appropriate civil disobedience. For without them, change certainly will never happen, and I encourage you to be guided by the thinking that: ***It's best to meet challenges with positive action, not negative reaction.***

As you contemplate the personal and professional choices in your life, now and in the future, these quotations from my journal may have value to you:

* ***Somerset Maugham: "It's a funny thing about life. If you refuse to accept anything but the best, you often get it."***

* ***George Bernard Shaw: "The people who get on in this world are those who look for circumstances they want, and if they can't find them, make them."***

* ***George S. Patton: "Accept the challenges so that you may feel the exhilaration of victory."***

* ***Mother Theresa: "Don't wait for others. Do it alone – person-to-person."***

JOURNAL 7

Preparation

"Chance favors the prepared mind."

– Louis Pasteur

It was my experience, and the experience of countless successful people I've read about, that preparation is fundamental to achieving success – in the workplace, and in life. It's too easy, and wrong, to attribute another's success simply to good luck, because:

"Luck is what happens when preparation meets opportunity."

– Elmer Letterman

Jennings Eldridge is the man I referred to in the Introduction, and I attribute so much of my success to the decades of mentoring I received from him. He said his preparation was guided by his journal entry: *I am my thoughts*.

Jennings said he knew his thoughts controlled his actions, and reactions, and he accepted the often harsh reality that: ***Everything happens for a reason.***

With Jennings guidance, these are some of the lessons I learned about preparation:

* I can train my mind to: ***Look forward with optimism and enthusiasm, and not backward with envy and regret.***
* It's my journey, and the decisions will be mine to make, but: ***If I insist on seeing things with perfect clarity before deciding, I never will.***
* I can almost always correct a wrong decision, guided by the knowledge that: ***More is lost through indecision than wrong decision.***
* My chances for success will be greatly enhanced if I: ***Focus on how something will work, not how it won't work.***
* From time to time, I'll second guess myself and my prior decisions, and: ***It's okay to recall mistakes I've made, as long as I also remember their lessons.*** But I shouldn't obsess over things I've said or done, because: ***The past is the past.***
* I am the pilot of my life, and: ***Every flight has a planned landing before takeoff.***
* Time is fleeting. With each new morning, I know: ***This day is the tomorrow I looked forward to yesterday.***
* As I prepare to embark on my new journey, I know I must be brave because: ***Fear will carry me further than courage, but not in the same direction.***

As Jennings did for me, I encourage you to think big thoughts and dream big dreams. And as you prepare to embark on your journey, you'll need to "suit up" for whatever your chosen profession or life's calling requires, knowing that: ***To leave my footprints in the sands of time, I must wear work boots.***

Success

**"Success is stumbling from failure to failure with no
loss of enthusiasm."**

– WINSTON CHURCHILL

PEOPLE FAR MORE QUALIFIED THAN me have written entire books on
this subject, and I encourage you to seek them out and read them –
as I have countless times during my career. When things weren't
going *my way,* as was often the case, and failure appeared inevitable,
I also drew strength each time I re-read passages about success in
my journals.

I shared with you my desire early in my professional life to create my
own company. Many of my journal entries fed that desire, but one in
particular, connecting athletic competition to other endeavors stood
out for me: ***The person with the ball determines if the motion is
forward or backward.***

Regarding your life, you have the ball, so you have control. But please remember: *Success comes from striving to win the game, not to just remain on the playing field.*

In striving to be successful, a lesson I learned the hard way was that while motivation can fade, habits will prevail, and: *It's easier to form good habits than to break bad ones.*

From what I've read, been told, observed and personally experienced, I know success:

- *is seldom convenient, or accidental*
- *requires no explanation, and failure permits no alibies*
- *is found by traveling a road always under construction*
- *involves the ruthless elimination of marginal opportunities*
- *may be determined more by what I don't do, than what I do*
- *requires determining the necessary, and blocking out the unnecessary*
- *comes not from knowing where I've been, or where I am, rather where I'm going*
- *comes from accepting that things don't have to be difficult or complex to be right*
- *comes from understanding not every ball thrown must be caught, not every question asked must be answered, and not every possible task must be performed*

What follows is one of the longest of all my journal entries, but one I felt compelled to share:

*"Nothing in the world can take the place of persistence.
Talent will not. Nothing is more common than unsuccessful
men with talent. Genius will not because unrewarded
genius is almost a proverb. Education will not since
the world is full of educated derelicts. Persistence and
determination are omnipotent."*

– *CALVIN COOLIDGE*

True North

"Live a purposeful life, not an accidental one."

– UNKNOWN

WHEN I WAS A HIGH school student, I did my homework at the kitchen table while my mother prepared dinner. She was always interested in my school work, so one evening I told her I was reading about *true north*. My textbook explained it was the direction of the North Pole relative to the navigator's position – a concept first discovered in 11th century China. She thought for a moment, then said, "I guess for us it would be heaven." I wrote my mother's words, not those in the textbook, in my journal later that night.

As I grew older, I came to believe the term also applied to a person who was there to guide me in the right direction. Until her death, my mother was "true north" to me. And there were three others in my life. Two were best friends from their childhood – my mentor, and my second husband. My first husband died of the same disease that will take me, but he brought me peace in accepting its inevitability when he spoke these true-north words:

*"I'm going to live each of my remaining days as
if it were my last so that when it happens, I'll be
proud of how I conducted myself, the things I
said and did."*

– BARREY KELLY

If you're a person of faith, then you have a true north to guide you.
I hope you're also blessed with true north in at least one mortal individual in your life. If not, perhaps beginning your journal will be a
step in that direction, being guided by the words of others. Here are
a few that impacted my life in a positive way:

* *"Yesterday is a cancelled check; tomorrow is a promissory
  note. Today is the only cash you have, so spend it wisely."
  –Kay Lyons*
* *"The quality of a person's life is in direct proportion to
  their commitment to excellence, regardless of their field of
  endeavor." –Vince Lombardi*
* *"Leaders are readers." –Unknown*
* *"When people talk, listen completely. Don't be thinking
  what you're going to say. Most people never listen." –Ernest
  Hemingway*
* *"For fast-acting relief, try slowing down." –Lily Tomlin*
* *"Fall seven times, stand up eight." –Japanese proverb*

Abraham Lincoln had more documented disappointments, failures
and tragedies than most historical figures of any generation, yet in
this quote, I believe he reveals a man who had found a true north in
his life:

"I do the best I know how, the very best I can. And I mean to keep on doing it to the end. If the end brings me out all right, what is said against me will not amount to anything. If the end brings me out all wrong, ten thousand angels swearing I was right would make no difference."

Different Drum

*"There is often value in turning left when
everyone else is going right."*

— **UNKNOWN**

DIFFERENT DRUM WAS THE TITLE of the first hit recording by one of
my favorite singers, Linda Ronstadt. And more than once I heard the
expression that a particular person was marching to the sound of a
different drum, meaning she or he was a non-conformist. We've all
encountered people we wish we could be more like, if only we weren't
held back by constraints we put on ourselves – in addition to those
imposed by others.

But I never believed it had to be all or nothing, and by living my
life *My Way*, I allowed myself to listen to, and occasionally march to,
a different drum. And so can you. Because of the unfair, and often
pervasive, reality of gender inequality, a previous journal entry spoke
only to available *workplace* choices. When charting the course of *all*
aspects of your life, you may be inspired by:

"One ship moves east and another west while the self-same wind blows. It's the set of the sail, not the gale, that bids them where to go."

– UNKNOWN

When I made choices about investing my time in any endeavor, I was guided by these words from Henry David Thoreau:

"The price of anything is the amount of life you will exchange for it."

My choices, personal and professional, were just that – mine. Not everyone can be, or should be, a business owner, a university president or a congresswoman. When thinking about your pursuit of your dreams, Booker T. Washington may have said it best:

"There is as much dignity in tilling the field as in writing a poem."

As you listen to that different drum while pursuing your dreams, let imagination be the cadence, because we all need fantasies to keep reality in perspective. Said another way:

"Those who don't believe in magic will never find it."

– ROALD DAHL

While most of my journal entries may be new to you, this inspiring one is likely familiar, and I believe it's usually attributed to Ralph Waldo Emerson:

> *"Do not follow where the path may lead. Go instead where there is no path and leave a trail."*

Inspiration

"The person who wins in life may have been
counted out several times, but he failed to
acknowledge the referee."

– H.E. JENSEN

AT THE BEGINNING, I SAID I didn't want this book to be about me, rather for you. And I certainly never wanted you to try to emulate me – except in two ways. I want you to begin to create journals, and to seek out and study inspirational role models who lift you up and accelerate the achievement of your dreams. It's important for you to emphasize the word *study*, rather than a cursory review, so you can truly learn about remarkable individuals of *your* choosing.

I chose mine from a variety of professions and walks of life. Education. Athletics. Politics. Entertainment. Religion. Philanthropy. Business. Government. Before you begin making your selections, I encourage you to first develop your own criteria of relevance to *you*, to *your life* and to *your dreams*.

I also encourage you to have as robust a list as possible, and keep adding to it. Expand your relevance "filter" when you come across someone whose life inspires you, even though their journey, and yours, appear to have little, if anything, in common. I'll share just a few of my recent examples to get you started, and none are from the world of business.

Although she's half my age, the most remarkable woman I've been inspired by in this or any year unquestionably is Jen Bricker. Her 2016 book is *Everything Is Possible,* and once you become acquainted with her life story, any obstacles in your life, real or imagined, will pale in comparison.

We lost Pat Summit last year. She was the record-setting women's basketball coach at the University of Tennessee. I encourage you to read her autobiography because her life story is inspiring in so many ways.

Carla Hayden's 2016 selection by the U.S. Senate to a ten-year renewable term to oversee the care and sharing of 162 million items in the world's largest library, the Library of Congress, is a first, both for a woman and an African-American woman.

The life journey of singer and actress Darlene Love has been especially inspirational to me.

Finally, I encourage you to be uplifted by the story of Misty Copland, who overcame challenges of poverty, discrimination and injury to recently become the first African-American female principal dancer with the American Ballet Theatre, one of America's three classical ballet companies.

Now it's your turn.

Become inspired, so you, in turn, can be a source of inspiration to others in the future. There's no reason why someday books won't be written by you, about you, or both.

Reflections

"Writing is thinking through the fingers."

− I*SAAC* A*SIMOV*

BECAUSE OF MY ILLNESS, I knew by the time I reached my twenties I had many more yesterdays than tomorrows.

God richly blessed me with the life I've lived, and I hope in some small way what I have shared with you from my journals, and my encouragement for you to begin your own journaling, will be a blessing in your life. The torch is passed.

It would have been a great joy to have met in person and discussed your dreams. Since that's not possible, I want to share a few final thoughts with you.

I believe with all my heart the things I wrote. Although life isn't fair, you can control *your* life and *your* dreams. Or not. It truly is a matter of choice. But even if you act with the best of intentions, guided by truth and honesty in all circumstances, and always with kindness and respect toward others, your life will not be trouble-free. Quite the opposite.

Early on, I accepted that adversity will always be with me. Many times, in my personal and professional life, I felt my coaches were all turning to pumpkins, and the darkness would never yield to dawn. But I always managed to survive the darkest days, the greatest challenges, and became a stronger person in the process. And I often discovered that what I was looking for, I was carrying with me all along. Seldom can we foresee adverse events, and we should have no expectation of a life without them. But we also should not expect the adversity will last, or that it will defeat us.

I hope you will embrace the journal idea in your own life. But if you don't, please find another form of familiar resources readily available to you in times of need, especially your *true north*.

I believe it was Will Rogers who said:

> **"Know what you're doing, love what you're doing, and
> believe in what you're doing."**

There were many times when I was uncertain I knew what I was doing. But there was never a time when I didn't love what I was doing. And I always believed in what I was doing. I hope you also have this wonderful experience of loving and believing in the path or paths you choose to take toward the realization of your dreams.

Communication is so important, in both our personal and professional lives. I'm concerned that the convenience of email and texting will inappropriately replace the spoken word, in person and on the phone, as well as words that could best be expressed in that most personal medium of one's own handwriting.

I didn't participate in social media, but for those who do, I offer this poem. I committed it to memory long ago, though I can't recall the author:

"Say it with flowers, say it with sweets; say it with kisses, say it with treats; say it with jewelry, say it with drink; but always be careful not to say it with ink."

I knew criticism was inevitable, and sometimes it was hurtful. When it came my way, I tried to first consider the source, then the circumstances. If appropriate, I made it a learning experience. If unjustified, I tried to follow words in my journal that said: **My best weapons against unjust criticism are a thick skin and short memory**, and then let it go and move on.

My instincts were never perfect, but I can't recall a single instance when initially giving everyone *the benefit of the doubt* was a mistake. And yet by doing so, wonderful things happened more often than not.

You are not alone in the world. It would be a rare individual, indeed, who doesn't care about the thoughts and impressions of others he or she encounters along life's journey. So it's important to remember: ***There is a difference between being noticed, and being remembered.*** Being noticed, of course, is far less enduring than being remembered, but it is *how* one is remembered that is the essence of this phrase.

There are things money can't buy. It's a long list, but among the more important ones, at least to me, are manners, morals, respect, character, common sense, trust, loyalty, patience, class, integrity and love.

I was often asked about the qualities of leadership. As you know, there are volumes of books on the subject, and some are excellent. I believe a leader should possess equal measures of courage and humility, and she should be publicly accountable for her performance against known goals and objectives. Leaders should strive to be someone others want to follow, even though they have no idea where she is going. What they *do* know is that accompanying her on her journey would be more gratifying than knowing the final destination.

History has shown that for anything truly great to be achieved, someone dreamed that it *should*, someone realized that it *could*, and someone believed that it *must*. Perhaps your dreams will be realized by being the "someone" participating in the actualization of the dreams of others.

We're both now at the end of *My Way*. It was a labor of love for me, but I've taken something of great value from you. Your time. And what you've invested can never be replaced. It's gone. I can only hope I've given you a measure of value in return.

I read somewhere a good speech is like a love letter because it's difficult to know where to begin or how to end because it comes from the heart. I've seldom given speeches, but writing this book has given me that understanding because it came from my heart.

At the beginning, I said, "I believe with all my heart that if I can, so can you." And as a person of faith, I also believe there is no scarcity in God's economy.

It is my fondest wish that you not go to your grave with your sweetest music left un-played. I don't believe I did.

Vaya Con Dios,
Mary Josephine Gilpin

AUTHOR NOTE

FOLLOW YOUR DREAMS AND *MY WAY* are works of fiction. Marla Jo Taylor and Mary Josephine Gilpin are fictional characters who came to life entirely from my imagination. However, it was my decades-long practice of journaling that was the inspiration for both books. All of Jo's *My Way* entries and quotes came from my journals.

As Jennings and Josephine did in the pages of fiction, I encourage you to embrace the practice of journaling as you go about your life in the real world. It can be life-changing. And you'll never know unless you try.

If this has been a pleasurable reading experience for you, I would be honored if you would post a review at Amazon.com. These reviews are vitally important to the marketing efforts of self-published authors, and it would mean so much to me. It will only take a few minutes, and there's a direct link from the "Buy" tab on my www. larrygildersleeve.com web site.

Thank you very much.

Larry B. Gildersleeve

ACKNOWLEDGEMENTS

As was true with my debut novel *Dancing Alone Without Music*, this sequel became a reality because of my wonderful writing coach and editor Lynda McDaniel. She guided me expertly and patiently through the process, and I'm deeply indebted to her. She lives in California, the sun rises for me in Kentucky, and we've never met. I hope that happens someday soon. Reverend Charles Flener was an enduring source of encouragement during my fifteen month journey from my first words to publication, and we're collaborating on a non-fiction book. Beverly Holland's review of my manuscript is acknowledged and greatly appreciated. Jenn Oliver continues as my professional proof-reader, and my virtual assistant is Lorraine Castle.

Cover design for *Follow Your Dreams* and *My Way* by Zebra Graphics, Bowling Green, KY.

Author photo by mandygarvinphoto.com

Larry B. Gildersleeve

Larry earned a BA degree in journalism and pre-law from Western Kentucky University, and an MBA from Indiana Wesleyan University. His dream to become a published author came true in 2016 with his debut novel, Dancing Alone Without Music. Larry and his wife Kathleen live in Bowling Green, Kentucky.

Contact
Facebook.com/LarryBGAuthor
larry@larrygildersleeve.com
www.larrygildersleeve.com